TRUE BLUE

DEBORAH ELLIS

pajamapress

The publisher gratefully acknowledges the support of the Canada Council for the
Arts and the Ontario Arts Council for its publishing program. We acknowledge
the financial support of the Government of Canada through the Book Publishing
Industry Development Program (BPIDP) for our publishing activities.

Canada Council   Conseil des Arts   ONTARIO ARTS COUNCIL
for the Arts   du Canada   CONSEIL DES ARTS DE L'ONTARIO

Library and Archives Canada Cataloguing in Publication

Ellis, Deborah, 1960-

　　True blue / Deborah Ellis.

ISBN 978-0-9869495-3-1 (bound).--ISBN 978-0-9869495-0-0 (pbk.)

　　I. Title.

PS8559.L5494T78 2011　　　　jC813'.54　　　　C2011-904883-3

U.S. Publisher Cataloging-in-Publication Data (U.S.)

Ellis, Deborah, 1960-
　　True blue / Deborah Eileen Ellis.
[231] p. : cm.
Summary: The darker side of a friendship is portrayed by Jess, a seventeen-year-old
who struggles to find the moral courage to remain loyal to her best friend Casey
who has been accused of murdering an eight year old girl at summer camp. The
town becomes a media circus and the pressures far too great for Jess to cope.
ISBN-13: 978-0-9869495-3-1
1. Friendship – Juvenile Fiction. 2. Peer pressure in adolescence – Juvenile fiction.
3. Conduct of life – Juvenile fiction. I. Title.
[Fic] dc22 PZ7.E469Tr 2011

Book and cover design–Rebecca Buchanan
Cover photo–Courtesy of John Spray
Insect images–Shutterstock

Pajama Press Inc.
469 Richmond St E, Toronto Ontario, Canada
www.pajamapress.ca

To those who have the courage to be friends.

Acknowledgements

I'd like to thank and acknowledge the contribution to this book of Gail Winskill, Ann Featherstone, Rev. Elaine Poproski and Heidy van Dyk.

ONE

Welcome to the Roach House.

Nobody calls it the Coach House, at least nobody local. You're not from around here, are you? Locals know better than to eat at this dump.

Still, it's the middle of the night and we're right off the highway. Any port in a storm, right?

Sit wherever. You have your pick of tables tonight.

Coffee? Coming up. It tastes like sludge, but it's hot and it'll keep you going. Take as long as you like to drink it. Take the rest of the night if you want.

You want some pie with that? The pie's safe. It comes from the bakery in the village. Rhubarb's the best. I can get you a slice...

Okay...why are you staring at me?

No, don't try to deny it. You're squinting at me, thinking to yourself, *where have I seen that face?*

…And now you've figured it out. Or maybe you've known it all along.

Yeah, I'm that girl.

My face was plastered all over the front pages and on TV. And don't get me started on the Internet. They've never let up, even after all this time.

It shouldn't have been this way. My life shouldn't have been dragged through the mud. After all, I wasn't even around when it happened.

I was the best friend, though. Fame by association. A person doesn't have to do anything special to become famous. It's enough to know someone who does.

Parasitic fame.

Casey would appreciate the parasitic reference. There are a lot of parasites in the insect world and she knows every one of them, Latin names and all. I was Dragonfly and she was Praying Mantis.

You know how the female praying mantis bites the head off the male when they're mating? That was our signal. You make a jaw out of your thumb and forefinger then bring them together fast. Like this—*snap*! It means, "This person is bothering me and deserves to have his head bitten off."

But you probably know all that from the newspapers.

We were just kids when we thought it up. Don't try to read anything into it—about her nature, I mean. She's not a violent person. Probably she doesn't ever call herself by that name anymore. But she used to. It was just a nickname. Just a little fun. But it was all put out there, for everyone to see. It's like my childhood isn't my own anymore.

I guess there's a lot you know. But there's a lot more you don't know.

You might as well get comfortable. Strap in, drink your coffee.

Because suddenly I feel like talking.

TWO

My best friend Casey was arrested for murder just as church was getting out.

The whole congregation was there to witness it.

We were spilled out over the sidewalk like monkeys from a barrel. The sun had finally started to shine again, hot and bright, after three days of rain. Steam rose from the sidewalk. The little park across the street looked deep green and clean, more like late spring than the last weekend of August.

We stood around in little groups, more subdued than usual. Kathy Glass, Stephanie's mother, was there. No one had expected her to come to the service. After all, Stephanie's body had only just been found. No one wanted to laugh or smile in front of her.

I was standing on the sidewalk with my parents and one of the deacons as they talked about church business.

It's a fluke that I was there. I'd had enough of God after spending six weeks as a camp counselor at Ten Willows. There we had church every Sunday in the outdoor chapel. We sang the Johnny Appleseed grace before every meal and when we had morning reflection, Bible study, and so on.

Do you know the Johnny Appleseed grace? I'll sing it for you.

Oh, the Lord is good to me,
And so I thank the Lord,
For giving me the things I need:
The sun and the rain and the apple seed.
The Lord is good to me.

We usually put in the word "dry" instead of "rain" because no one wants it to rain for camp. We didn't do that during the last camp. The summer had been very dry and we needed the rain. Maybe we should have kept calling for dry.

I don't usually go to church. But I knew Stephanie — more than I wanted to—so when she turned up dead, it seemed like the right thing to do.

Plus, my mother insisted.

Two police cars were waiting at the curb. At first

I didn't give them a thought. The police stayed inside their cars until Casey came out of church with her family. They were always among the last to leave because of her father's wheelchair. He liked to wait until most of the people were gone so he didn't have to maneuver it through the crowd.

Out of the corner of my eye I could see Casey and her parents approach Reverend Fleet, who stood by the open doors for the ritual post-service handshake. It was strange for me to see Casey in a dress after weeks in camp clothes.

Reverend Fleet shook hands with Mr. and Mrs. White, but when he got to Casey he did something different. He grabbed hold of her arm and placed his hand on her head, like he was praying over her.

Knowing how Casey felt about the pompous old reverend, I'm sure she wished she were truly a praying mantis at that moment, able to snap off his head in a single gulp. I'm sure she wished that a swarm of killer bees would fly up his robe and send him dancing and screaming down the street.

I started paying attention when three cops got out of their cars. We all did. It was like that moment of silence after the sermon when the minister finally stops talking that signals the congregation to wake up, it's time to hand over the offering. Everyone stopped their chitchat and turned toward the open door of the church. The traffic stopped rolling and the birds stopped singing, and everyone clearly heard the words of the police officer, who stepped up to my friend.

"Casey White, you are under arrest for the murder of Stephanie Glass."

Casey's arms were pulled behind her back. We heard a quick series of clicks as the handcuffs were secured around her wrists.

The TV crews came out of nowhere. They filmed the cops taking Casey down the church steps to the police car. When they showed it later on the national news, there was a blurry spot over her face so she couldn't be identified, since she was only seventeen. But everyone in town knew it was her. There are nine thousand people in Galloway and everyone knows practically everyone else. Word got around, and quickly.

We all watched the cop put her in the back seat of the car and hold the top of her head so she wouldn't bang it on the doorframe. No one moved. No one tried to talk them out of it. We all just let it happen.

The car was pulling away from the curb when Casey's mother sprang forward, just in time to land her fists on the trunk. Her cry must have been heard clear across town.

"Nooooooo!"

Casey's father tried to get down the wheelchair ramp, but there were people blocking his way. They were all watching Mrs. Glass talk into the TV microphones, saying she was grateful to the police for making such a quick arrest.

By the time Mr. White finally made it down the ramp, he and his wife could only stare together down the road. My mother went up to them and said something comforting, but I don't think they heard her.

Me?

I stayed where I was. And watched.

Until Mom stomped past me.

"Let's go," she barked.

I had to run to catch up.

I'm in grade three the first time I notice Casey.

It's the end of recess. The bell rings and we all line up, yelling and pushing. Except for Casey. She's standing still, her hands cupped in front of her, holding a large green insect.

"What's that?" a girl asks, then screeches, "Ewww!"

A lot of girls start to shriek, the way girls do. They run around, and then the boys run, and everyone scatters across the playground.

I don't run. I just watch.

Ms. Thackeray has a hard time rounding them up again.

"That thing belongs on the playground," she snarls at Casey.

"It's a praying mantis," Casey says. "I found it in the bushes."

"Then you can just put it back in the bushes."

"After I look at it for a while."

Casey doesn't ask. She just says. I've never heard a kid talk like that to an adult before. Not asking. Not whining. Just saying. As if what she wants is as important as what the teacher wants.

Casey walks right past Ms. Thackeray and into the school. She makes it into the classroom before Ms. Thackeray catches up with her. The teacher grabs her arm and the praying mantis goes flying around the room. All the kids scream and carry on.

The bug finally lands on Nathan Ivory's

desk. Nathan smashes it with a book. Casey shoves him so hard he skids across the floor, knocks his face into a bookshelf, and bloodies his nose. Casey tries to pick up the pieces of the insect. Ms. Thackeray drags her away to the principal's office.

After that, kids start calling Casey the Praying Mantis.

Casey loves it.

And we become friends. She likes me because I don't squeal like an idiot at the sight of a bug. I don't love bugs like Casey does, but I don't see any reason to get worked up about them. Casey doesn't care that no one else wants to be my friend. And I like that she likes me.

THREE

Mom got on the phone the minute we walked through the door.

"You release that girl this instant! What do you mean by arresting her in front of the whole town like that? Did you even think about her poor parents? Well, it's your department I feel sorry for, because you are going to be hit with such a lawsuit—"

The cop at the other end of the phone let Mom rant. A wise move. Mom's a ranter, even when she's not ill. She has to get that first rush of adrenalin out of her system when she's angry. Only then can she discuss something halfway calmly. Unless she's ill. When she's ill, there's no calming her down. I listened for the tell-tale shrillness but didn't hear it. She was just angry.

She kept on being angry. From the short spurts of silence, I could tell the cop was getting a few words in here and there, but Mom was still fuming when she hung up the phone.

"And I didn't do anything!" she wailed—in my direction but really to herself. "I didn't try to stop them!"

"It was all over in a few seconds," my father pointed out as he undid his necktie. My father always spoke in a bland voice to counteract my mother's wildness. "There was no time for any of us to react. And what could we do—take her away from the police? They'll realize they've made a mistake and let her go."

Mom hadn't yet wound down to her rational stage, so I knew Dad's comments would be wasted. I went up to my room and shut the door. I had enough of my own emotions to sort out without taking on Mom's as well.

I hung up my church dress then sat down on my unmade bed. Camp was over. There was no need to tidy my bunk for cabin inspection, like I had every morning for the past eight weeks. There were no little campers to bully into doing likewise.

None of my regular clothes were clean. Not a single pair of shorts, not one t-shirt. Camp had ended three days before, but I still hadn't tackled my enormous bag of laundry. Casey had done hers at camp. She had far fewer clothes than I did. She washed them out every night in the bathroom and hung them to dry on the clothesline outside the cabin, or on the end of her bunk if the weather was bad.

"I've got to learn to live in the field," she once said to me as she rinsed out her socks.

"Have at it," I replied. "I'm going to be a gym teacher, not an entomologist. I'll live in a house with a washing machine and spend my free time adding up my pension. You'll spend your life crawling in the dirt and drying the same three pairs of socks in the smoke of your campfire."

"Jealousy is unbecoming," she said, flicking water at me from a clean, wet sock.

Casey is orderly. She's a scientist. I'm a jock. I'm a mess.

I mean I was a jock. Now I don't know what I am.

And, to tell the truth, I wasn't much of a jock. To be a real jock you have to care about winning—and winning took too much effort.

I didn't really want to be a gym teacher, either. People were always asking me what I wanted to be. I had to tell them something so they'd leave me alone.

The only clothing I had that was remotely clean was a pair of pajamas. I put them on, then picked up my duffel bag and hauled it down to the basement. I emptied it out onto the laundry-room floor.

There it was, the whole summer spread out before me—shorts from hot days, jeans from campfire nights, socks with grass stains, t-shirts with little splats of blood from mosquitos slapped too late. I held a sweatshirt up to my face. It smelled of wood smoke.

I didn't bother to sort out the light clothes from dark. They were camp clothes. They were used to rough treatment.

I shoved as much laundry as I could into the washer. The noise of the machine muffled the sound of my mother's voice. I closed the basement door to block out the rest. Then I sat down in the beat-up chair we keep in the laundry room—one of Mom's "projects." She'd always meant to take an upholstery class and redo it. Casey's father offered to help her, since that's one of the things he did for a living, but she could never decide on what fabric to use.

Our laundry room was also a storage room. The shelves were full of projects my mother had started then abandoned but couldn't part with. My own past was there, too—a guitar, a chess set, an easel and some dried-up acrylics, a tennis racket, lots of things that didn't work out. My parents kept encouraging me. Casey kept encouraging me. It was all really annoying.

I listened to the *thwack-thwack* of the washing machine and thought about how strange it was to be doing ordinary things while my best friend was in jail for murder.

Then I remembered. Casey was supposed to go to Australia in December for four months. She'd been accepted on some professor's field team to study insects there. It was a big deal for someone still in high school.

I guess you won't be going to Australia now, Praying Mantis, I thought. She wouldn't be leaving me on my own after all.

Something else nagged at me, something I couldn't quite name. It didn't feel good.

I didn't want to think anymore, so I went upstairs to get something to eat.

"Close the door," Mom said, as she always did when I stood in front of an open fridge. "We don't need to refrigerate the whole house."

I took out the milk and closed the door. Mom hadn't made anything for lunch. In fact, she was still in her church clothes. I decided on bread and peanut butter.

Mom was glaring at the phone.

"What's wrong?" I asked.

"You think you know a town," she replied. "You think you know the people in it, and the things they stand for, and the lines of decency they will not cross. Then something like *this* happens."

"What's wrong?" I asked again.

"I've called ten people from our church, ten people

who have known the Whites since they came to this town. None of them will go down to the police station with me."

"You're going to the police station?"

"And that Reverend Fleet! He said he would pray for them!"

"Isn't that his job?"

"His *job* is to come down to the police station with me and help correct this terrible injustice. Jesus Christ the Lord could be in that cell and Reverend Fleet would not put himself out. I told him that. And do you know what he said? He said, 'Kathy Glass is a member of our community, too.' As if one has anything to do with the other!"

I took a bite of my sandwich. The peanut butter gobbed up in my mouth. I had to wash it down with a big gulp of milk.

"I wonder what Casey's having for lunch," I said. "Maybe we should take her some sandwiches."

Mom looked at me, hard, with one of her deep, searching looks. "Jessica Jude, why aren't you more upset about this?"

"I am upset," I said. "I'm just...stunned, is all."

"Well, get unstunned," she snapped. "Being stunned won't help your friend."

Mom turned back to the phone book.

I chewed on my sandwich and listened to her try to persuade people to go to the police station with her. She wasn't clear what they would do once they got there, other than demand the police let Casey go. It wasn't much of a plan, but that's Mom.

Of course the plan went nowhere.

"We need a nickname for you," Casey says to me one day when we are playing in the patch of meadow near the schoolyard. She is looking at a blue dragonfly that has perched on her arm. "What kind of things do you like?"

I don't know. I'm not really all that interested in anything. I just pass through each day as it comes to me.

When I don't answer, she looks up at me.

"You're wearing the same color," she says.

I don't understand, and then I look at the dragonfly. She's right. We are wearing the same shade of blue.

"We can call you Dragonfly," she suggests.

And Dragonfly becomes my nickname.

That night, I woke up when the bedroom was still dark. My clock radio read two a.m. I tried to get back to sleep, but I couldn't get comfortable.

Ride your bike, a voice inside my head kept saying. I tried reading, but not even that would shut the voice up. Tired of struggling, I rolled out of bed and dressed.

Mom is a light sleeper, even when she isn't ill. The last thing I wanted was to wake her up. I cringed at every squeak in the floor but managed to get outside without her coming out of her room.

I'd never been biking at that hour of the morning. The town was quiet. I biked from street to street, feeling like the only person awake in the whole world.

I biked over to the police station and circled around and in front of the place where Casey was being held. I imagined her chained to a dungeon wall. Then I imagined her being so busy examining the fleas and lice in the cell that she didn't even notice the chains. That image made me smile.

It occurred to me what that feeling was—the feeling that had been nagging at me ever since I'd watched Casey being taken away.

I was stuck here in a normal life, in boring old Galloway. Casey had been whisked up into something new, away from me. While I was doing chores and getting ready for school, she was surrounded by excitement, the center of attention. Casey had left me behind.

I was all alone.

And I didn't like it one bit.

We are in grade seven, spending the afternoon at Ten Willows on a warm September Saturday. It is off-season at the camp, so we have the place to ourselves.

Casey is watching a spider suck the blood out of a fly. She is completely absorbed.

After a while, she says, "I'm going to need to specialize. There are so many insects—over a million different species have been identified. I can't possibly learn about all of them! I could specialize in spiders, but I don't think so. And I don't think it's butterflies, either. Beetles? I like beetles. A lot. Maybe beetles. But which beetles? There are so many different ones."

I am bored. "Let's do something," I say.

"I am doing something," she replies. "Look, you can actually see the spider's fangs! I think it's eating an anthomyiid fly."

I pick up a stick and swirl it through the web, ripping it apart. Then I fling it all away.

"She wasn't finished her lunch," Casey says.

"Let's do something!"

"You need a hobby," Casey says. She walks away to look for another bug.

She sounds just like my mother. I am so upset I walk away from her. Then I start running. I run and run, all around the camp trails, just to get away. When I get back to where I started, Casey isn't there.

She's gone looking for me, I think, feeling smug that I've made her break off her bug search. I sit, panting from my run, and then decide to go looking for her.

It takes a while.

I find her kneeling on the boardwalk that leads through the marsh. She is looking down at whirligig beetles and pond skaters. She is gently prodding the pond skaters with a thin reed and watching them skim over the surface of the water.

She looks up at the sound of my sneakers on the boardwalk.

"Isn't this amazing?" she says. "All these different forms of life in one small space—bugs and spiders and birds and plants. I think maybe this is it. I think maybe I'll specialize in aquatic insects."

"I've been running," I tell her. "All over camp."

"That's it," she says. "You should be a cross-country runner."

FOUR

The day after Casey was arrested was Labor Day. I wanted to sleep in, not just because it was the last day of the summer holiday and school was starting the next day, but because I'd been out riding my bicycle at the crack of stupid. But it was barely eight o'clock in the morning when the cop came knocking.

Our house was one of those small, squished-together ranchers. Casey's was the same. My bedroom window was right beside the front door, so I could hear Mom open up.

"I'd like to speak to your daughter Jessica," a female voice said. "Is she here?"

I recognized the voice. It was Detective Ann Bowen. She was the chief investigating officer during Stephanie's last disappearance.

"Why do you need to talk to Jude?" my mother asked. "You should be out looking for that little girl's killer, because the girl you've got locked up did not do it!"

Then I heard my dad's voice, calm and bland.

"Won't you come in?" he said. "I'll get Jess."

I jumped out of bed just as Dad rapped on my door. I told him I'd be right out. I threw some clothes on and dashed into the bathroom to splash water on my face and pull myself together. As I came out of the bathroom I heard Mom talking to the cop in the kitchen.

"Her father called her Jessica after Jessica Lang — he's had a crush on her since *Tootsie*. I called her Jude because of the Beatles song." Mom was pouring coffee when I came into the kitchen. "Here's my Jude. She'll help you any way she can. Casey White is her best friend."

Mom came over to me and started to smooth down my hair, but I pulled away from her and took a seat at the table.

Detective Bowen nodded her greeting, but I didn't like the way she was looking at me.

"I don't know what I can help you with," I said. "I wasn't there."

"Just one or two things," Detective Bowen said.

"I really don't have anything else to say."

"Should I call our lawyer?" my father asked. That's Dad, cautious to the bone.

"Your daughter is in no way a suspect in Stephanie's murder," Detective Bowen said. "You are free to call a lawyer if you want to, but there's no need. Jess, I know you want to help your friend. There are still a few little points you can help us understand. Will you do this for Casey?"

"She will," my mother said.

Detective Bowen kept her eyes on me.

"Of course," I said. "Anything to help Casey."

"Good." Detective Bowen smiled. The smile didn't reach her eyes. "Could you tell me a bit about Casey's relationship with Stephanie?"

She took a minirecorder out of her pocket and placed it on the table in front of me. She also took out her notebook and pen.

"Are you all right with me recording what your daughter has to say?" she asked my parents. "As I get older, my memory gets weaker."

My father hemmed a bit but my mother overrode him.

The cop asked for my permission, too, but I couldn't think of a good reason to say no.

"Casey's relationship with Stephanie," she prompted.

"She was Stephanie's camp counselor."

"And?"

"That's it."

"How did they get along?"

"They got along fine. They weren't close or anything, but there were seven other kids in our cabin. They all needed our attention."

Detective Bowen tapped her pen on the table. "So you're saying there was no special tension between Casey and Stephanie."

"That's right."

"You know, Jess, you seem to be a smart young woman, but what you are doing now is very stupid."

"There's no need—," my father began.

I started to tremble and crossed my legs to control it. "I don't know what you mean."

"Giving contradictory statements to the police. Makes me think I can't trust you."

"Jude, what is she talking about?" my mother asked.

Detective Bowen stared at me. Her stare was even harder than my mother's, and I couldn't meet it.

"In our earlier conversations, just after Stephanie's disappearance was reported, and over the course of the search, you frequently spoke of how annoying Stephanie was, how she'd steal things and disrupt the group. And now you're saying that Stephanie was a model camper and Casey was a model counselor."

"Casey *was* a model counselor! You try keeping kids amused all summer without TV, computers, or video games. Casey is amazing at that, much better than me. To me, it's just a job. The pay is lousy but it's more fun than working at Burger World. For Casey, it's something more."

"Tell me."

"It was…" I searched for the right word. The only one I could find had a churchy feel to it, but it seemed right. "It was a mission. Like bugs is her mission. She could take a kid who was deathly afraid of bugs, and by the end of camp that kid would be letting spiders and beetles crawl all over her. She says that girls get stronger when they learn to handle bugs, because it means they are breaking the mold that's been cast for them. Snakes, too. Ask her. She can explain it better than I can. She also believes there's something magical about camp, that ten days at camp can make everything right with every kid."

"It didn't work that way with Stephanie, did it?" Detective Bowen asked.

After a moment, I answered. "No."

"As a matter of fact, the longer camp went on, the worse Stephanie seemed to get, isn't that right?"

"Casey tried so hard!" I suddenly felt like crying— my face hurt from the effort to hold it back.

"Someone as dedicated as Casey would keep trying," Detective Bowen said. "She'd go the extra mile and beyond."

"Casey White is an extraordinary girl," Mom interjected. "Disciplined. Dedicated. Honorable. And a joy to be around. Did you know she's been accepted to join a field study this December on Lord Howe Island off the coast of Australia? Her family's not rich. She has to cover her travel expenses. She could have found a higher-paying job for the summer—really, any business in town would have loved to hire her. But she had already committed to Ten Willows. 'I'll just get a job after school,' she told me. That girl is not afraid of hard work!"

I wanted Mom to shut up. I'd heard that Industrious-Casey speech way too often.

Detective Bowen poured some more milk into her coffee mug and took a long time to stir it.

"Is there anything else?" I finally asked.

Detective Bowen looked at me and smiled a little. She could tell she'd gotten to me.

"Did Casey ever lose her temper with Stephanie?"

"Casey has never lost her temper," Mom said. "Not once."

"Jessica?" Detective Bowen prompted. "We've already talked to the girls from your cabin."

"Then why are you asking me?"

"Detective, if you already have the information, why do you need to hear it again from Jess?" my father asked. "All this has been hard on her, too."

"I'm just trying to get a complete picture of what happened."

"I don't have to answer your questions if I'm not

under arrest," I said. "And not even then. I remember that from law class in grade eleven."

"I thought you wanted to help your friend."

"How can this be helping? You're looking for negative things! Everybody gets mad at kids. Kids make you mad. That's what they do. Not all kids and not all the time, but they make you mad!"

I got up from the table and fiddled with the orange juice container on the counter, just to get away from her.

"Let's leave that topic, then," the detective said. "A t-shirt of Stephanie's was found in Casey's duffel bag. Any idea how it got there?"

I was facing the counter, not the table. I felt myself stiffen up. I poured the juice into a glass.

"How would I know that?" I asked.

"It was a t-shirt that everyone assumed she was wearing when she disappeared. It had Tinker Bell on the front of it. Do you remember it?"

I took a swallow of orange juice and turned back to face the table.

"A lot of girls wore Tinker Bell shirts this summer."

"Her mother said it was her favorite. It wasn't among her belongings and she wasn't wearing it when her body was found. But it turned up in Casey's bag. With bloodstains on it. Both Stephanie's and Casey's blood."

"Kids get injured at camp," I said. "Scraped knees

31

when they fall, scratched cheeks from flapping branches on trail hikes. Casey and I carried little first aid kits on our belts."

"So you know nothing about Stephanie's t-shirt? Because Casey said you must have put it in her bag, that you were doing the cabin cleanup while she was out with the search party. So I'm asking you. Did you put it in her duffle bag?"

"Of course she didn't," Mom said. "Why would she put a child's t-shirt into her friend's bag? Why would she do that?"

"Maybe it was an accident." Detective Bowen's voice was calm in contrast to the shrillness of Mom's. "Maybe Jess was in a hurry. Maybe there was a lot to do and not much time to do it. I'm not saying she was malicious. Maybe she was just careless."

At the word *careless* Mom's head jerked back to look at me. My legs started to shake again. I sat down quickly.

"Did you do that?" Mom asked me. "Because that sounds like you." She turned back to Detective Bowen. "I keep finding soup tins in the garbage can. The recycling box is right there, but she won't take two seconds to rinse the can out and drop it in. Won't take two seconds to help the environment. Casey—"

I saw Dad put his hand on Mom's wrist to shut her up. I was grateful. She was about to talk about Casey getting the Mayor's Environmental Award for a campaign she led to turn a trash heap over by the old underwear factory into a nature park. I didn't need to hear about it again.

"Is that what happened?" Detective Bowen asked me. "And I want you to think before you answer. If Casey gets convicted because of that shirt in her bag, and she is innocent, it means that Stephanie's real killer is still out there, maybe getting ready to kill someone else. My job is to track down a murderer based on the evidence. And so far, all the evidence is pointing to Casey. If I'm wrong, I want to know. I also want you to think carefully, because there is such a thing as obstructing police in the commission of an investigation. It's a criminal charge, and lying to the police could be seen as obstruction."

"That's enough," my father said. "There's no need for that. If Jessica says she didn't do it, then she didn't do it."

"I haven't heard her say she didn't."

That was my cue. All eyes turned toward me.

"I didn't do it," I heard myself say. "I didn't do it."

August 22

Day 1

It's opening day of the last camp of the summer.

Swarms of girls are crowded into the mess hall with their parents, handing over doctors' notes and getting assigned to cabins. I recognize some girls from previous years. The repeaters are easy to spot. They are laughing, greeting their friends, squirming away from their parents. The newbies are also easy to spot. They stand close to Mummy and Daddy, looking scared and lost. Some are crying.

When I first spot Stephanie Glass I don't give her a second look.

I sort of know her from church. I've seen her singing in the junior choir and I've seen the back of her head as she goes down the aisle to the front of the church for the children's story and then on to Sunday school. I know her father is dead. Heart attack? Cancer? Whatever. She and her mother sit on the opposite side of the church from my parents, and our families are not friends.

Her being at camp is no surprise. Lots of local kids go. So I ignore her. I am on the lookout for

the eight-year-olds I think will be in our cabin.
Stephanie looks older than eight.

Casey is standing behind the registration table,
ready to immediately greet any kid assigned to
Cabin Three. I sit on a bench along the side of
the hall, watching and waiting for the kids to
come to me. I figure I'll see more than enough of
them over the next ten days.

I'm glad this is the last camp of the summer.
I like Ten Willows best when it is just Casey and
me. But all summer we've been junior counselors
assigned to someone else's cabin. For this camp,
one of the senior counselors dropped out at the
last minute, and we are finally together.

"If I let the two of you lead a cabin on your
own," said Mrs. Keefer, the camp director, "do you
think you can manage to keep the campers alive?"

"Alive and happy," Casey said. "Really, we can
do this."

Of course we can do this, I think, as I watch
the camper chaos sort itself out. We've been

coming to Ten Willows since we were children—camp in the summer, youth weekends in the winter, leadership training, endless volunteer hours cleaning and painting when camp is out.

After everything we've done for this camp, I figure we are owed this time to hang out together.

If only the campers don't get in the way too much.

Casey appears in front of me with eight little girls in tow, including Stephanie. She stands out from the rest. She looks like a doll in her Tinker Bell t-shirt, or an ornament on a cake. She knows it, too. The other girls are looking at Casey and me to see what we will tell them to do next. Stephanie is checking out her reflection in the glass of the camp craft display case, twirling her blonde hair into ringlets.

We load up with bedrolls and backpacks and head off to our cabin. By the time everyone finds their assigned bunks, chooses the cabin name (the Butterflies) and listens to Casey and me go over the camp rules, it's time to get ready for lunch.

We herd the kids outside the cabin and Casey does a body count. She comes up one body short and blows two short blasts on her whistle.

"Buddies!" she calls out.

We've paired them up. Alison, Stephanie's buddy, is alone.

"Where's Stephanie?"

We all look around the cabin and in the washrooms, calling her name but seeing no sign of her. She pops up twenty minutes later.

"I had no idea you were looking for me," she says, smiling sweetly and tossing her hair.

We laugh it off. Except for the cold grilled-cheese sandwiches we have to endure, and the Johnny Appleseed grace we have to sing in front of the whole camp, there are no other consequences.

She disappears again after lunch, cutting into the Butterflies' swim time by fifteen minutes. After swimming, we spend another fifteen minutes shivering in our wet bathing suits, looking for Stephanie. Casey finally spots her hiding behind a canoe, watching us and laughing.

"You need to stay with us," Casey tells her. "We need to know where you are. You don't want to keep everybody waiting, do you?"

"If she wants to hide, let's let her hide," I tell Casey. "She'll get tired of it if we ignore her."

But Casey is determined to win her over. She tries talking with her before lights out.

"We want to get to know you," she tells Stephanie. "How can we do that if you keep running off?"

"I don't care if you get to know me or not," Stephanie says. "And it's your job to keep track of me, not my job to keep track of you."

Casey doesn't give up.

"You need to stay with the group because we're going to do all sorts of fun things. If you're not with us, you'll miss out, and we want you to have a really great time at this camp."

Little Stephanie just smiles sweetly and chirps, "I am having a good time."

FIVE

"That's enough," my father said. "I don't like your tone. If there's anything else you want to know, I'd like our lawyer to be present. We'll come to the station."

"That's not necessary," Mom said, but my father ushered Detective Bowen out the door, which he closed and locked behind her. He used the phone in the kitchen to call Gerald Grey, his golfing buddy and lawyer. All the time he was talking, I kept my eyes on my orange juice because I knew my mother had her eyes on me.

"He'll meet us at the police station in one hour." Dad made his announcement, then retreated to his basement office.

I pushed back my chair and went to my room. But I couldn't stay there because I was afraid Mom would come in and I'd be trapped. I had to get out. But I'd have to go by the kitchen, which was at the center of the house. No escape through either the front or back door without going past her.

I paced back and forth.

My bedroom was small. There was room for a single bed, a desk, and a dresser—that was all. I'd rearranged it a dozen different ways over the years, but nothing gave me more space.

Casey's room wasn't any bigger, but her father had built her a bug lab in the garage, so she hung out there most of the time.

There was no extra space for me in my house. We had another bedroom, larger than mine, which my mother used for all her crafts and projects. She did a lot of shift work at the nursing home and rarely slept when my father and I did. When she did sleep, it was on a single cot beside her projects. My father slept in their bedroom, surrounded by the same matching set they'd bought when they were first married. Once a year my father took out the tin of wood wax and rubbed it until it shone.

My bedroom furniture was bought when I graduated from the crib. It was grown-up furniture, the same style as my parents' bedroom set, solid and unbreakable. Once I put Snow White stickers on the drawers of the desk. I had to spend three hours steaming them off and applying a new coat of wax, under my father's supervision.

"Good things will last if you take care of them," he said. "This furniture will still look like new when you leave here and set up your own home." I was five at the time and had no notion of leaving, but when he said that, it felt like I was already halfway out the door.

I paced around in the few feet of space between the bed and the dresser, and thought about Casey, pacing back and forth in her cell.

And then I had another thought—a thought that would fix everything and bring Casey back. She'd be so happy, and her parents would be so happy, that they would all let me go to Australia with her.

I would rescue Casey from jail.

I would bike to the police station, burst in there, and create some kind of diversion like setting off the fire alarm. And while all the cops were running around like chickens with no heads, I'd pull Casey out of her cell and we'd hit the road. We'd find a good hiding place and lay low for a bit. Stephanie's real killer would be found, and life would go back to normal.

Did I think the police would just run for their lives

and leave the prisoners in their cells? Was I picturing a cell out of a Wild West jail, where the key hung from a nail just outside the cell door? I don't know what I was thinking. I was a little crazy, at that moment.

Crazy or not, at least it made me feel bold enough to leave my bedroom, stride past my disapproving mother with a quick, "I'll meet you there," and head out on my bike.

My bike wasn't really my bike. It was my father's bike, but he no longer rode it. I used to have my own bike, a very nice one—a silver Schwinn, very sleek, very expensive. I used to have a lot of expensive things. Mom would buy them for me on mad shopping sprees. She'd max out the credit cards. I'd use the things until she crashed, then Dad would return what he could and sell the rest to keep us from drowning in debt. When I was younger I thought my father was always angry with me, the way he took away the nice things my mother gave me. It was years before I understood.

It felt good to be moving, but I had forgotten about the Galloway Labor Day parade. I started off pedaling at full steam but ran smack into roadblocks and baton-twirlers. I had to try several different routes, and by the time I managed to navigate my way through to the right area of town, I felt shaky and uncertain, a little freaked out about the whole thing. By the time I got to the police station, I was less and less sure about my plan.

I rode around and around in the parking lot, getting sweaty both from the sun and from the thought of the magnitude of what I was about to do. I wanted to keep biking until my nerves caught up with my ideas, but I started getting funny looks from people at the Dairy Queen next door. Also, time was passing, and my parents would be at the station soon. If I was going to act, it had to be now. Even then, I almost biked away. But I said to myself, "No, you never stick to anything, You're not leaving here without at least trying to do what you came here to do."

I locked my bike to the chain-link fence and went into the police station. I'd find a fire alarm, pull it, and then go hide until the building had cleared out. After that, it would be easy to get to the cells and let Casey out.

I started to feel lucky because there was a fire alarm pull station right inside the foyer, right beside the rack of leaflets about elder abuse.

I raised my hand to get ready to pull the alarm, then I realized it wasn't the same kind we had at school. I didn't know how to work this one and had to lean in to read the instructions, which were written in tiny print. I was almost at the point of figuring it out when the door opened.

"Just grab and pull." Detective Bowen stood in the

doorway. "Is there a fire?"

"I just wanted…" I grabbed a leaflet with a sad old woman's face on the front.

"School project?" Detective Bowen asked.

I nodded.

"Well, good luck with that."

She went back into the station. I turned and went out of it, back into the sunshine. It took me a full minute to remember that school hadn't started yet, so I couldn't have a school project. Detective Bowen had been laughing at me.

I thought about leaving right then and not answering any more of her questions. And I would have left, but just at that moment my parents and their lawyer pulled into the parking lot. I held the door open for my mom.

"You could have changed your shirt," Mom said as she walked past me.

The lawyer didn't say anything. Dad took hold of the door and motioned for me to go in before he did. He didn't say anything, either, but he did put his hand on my shoulder for a second. It wasn't much but it was something.

August 22

Day 1, Evening

Casey and I take our problem to the Counselors'
Council. The Council is a quick meeting held each
evening after the campers are in bed to sort out
issues and plan programs.

The counselors who have been there all
summer are too tired to get very excited about
Stephanie's behavior.

"I'll trade you your vanisher for my bed
wetter," one of them says.

"Can we make all the kids disappear?"

The counselors who are fresh because they'd
arrived later in the season, look smug—so far, all
their kids are behaving.

"Encourage her to join in," Mrs. Keefer says.
"Camp is supposed to be fun. Redirect the child.
Help her feel like she wants to be part of the
group. Try giving her some responsibility. And I'll
have a talk with her."

"Couldn't we just call her mother?" I ask. "I don't want Mrs. Glass blaming us if her precious daughter gets lost in the woods."

Mrs. Keefer sighs then nods. The Council ends and Casey and I go with her to her office, a little room off the mess hall. She finds Stephanie's registration form, dials the number, listens to the answering machine on the other end then hangs up without leaving a message.

"Mrs. Glass has gone to visit her brother in Regina for the week," she says. "No point in bothering her out there. She left a local emergency contact—Stephanie's aunt—but this is hardly an emergency. Stephanie is here with us, and it's up to us to see that she doesn't get lost in the woods."

She says this last bit while peering over her glasses at me. Casey is the one who hears her. I'd be happy if the little brat were to disappear and stay that way. Less work.

"We'll give her more attention," she says to me

as we head back to our cabin.

"It's a waste of time," I say.

But she doesn't listen to me. She talks on and on about ways we can get Stephanie engaged with the group and feeling excited about being in camp. She is certain that her way of dealing with the kid will work.

Casey always does just what she wants to do.

Maybe it's different in big cities, but the police station in our small town looked nothing like the police stations on television. Mr. Grey gave our names to the desk clerk, then we all sat on plastic orange chairs and waited. I started to leaf through an old copy of *Reader's Digest* that had been left on the empty chair next to me, but Mom hissed at me to put it down and I didn't feel like arguing with her.

The desk clerk must have given some signal to the lawyer, because we all got to our feet and headed down a hall and into a small room. We took seats around a table. When I looked up, I saw myself reflected in the one-way mirrors that lined one side of the room.

Detective Bowen came in, shook hands with Mr. Grey, and got right down to business.

"You and Casey know the property at the Ten Willows Camp quite well, don't you? In fact, you often go there even when there is no camp in session."

"We've been doing that for years," I said. "We have permission."

"I know you do. You are both trusted and thought of very highly by the camp administration. What do you do out there, just the two of you?"

The best times I've ever had in my life were when Casey and I were alone at the camp, but the private life of Dragonfly and Praying Mantis were none of Detective Bowen's business.

"We hiked, had picnics, things like that. Casey looked for bugs and I trained. I'm on the cross-country team at school."

"You both know the trails?"

"We can do them with our eyes closed. As a matter of fact, we're going to trying walking on one of the trails blindfolded later this fall. That is, we planned to."

"Who came up with that idea?"

"Casey. She suggested it when we were on a pause during the hike to the sleep-out area."

"Is that the pause you were on because Stephanie disappeared again?"

I nodded. "That's right. We were taking the kids across the creek on an old log that acts as a bridge.

It's not high but to little kids, it can be scary at first. When we got everyone to the other side, we did a body count. Stephanie was missing again. She reappeared ten minutes later, the way she always did. While we were waiting, we talked about how well we knew the trails, especially the Willow Trail, which was the one we were on. That's when Casey came up with the idea."

"When Stephanie disappeared, you didn't go looking for her right away?" Detective Bowen asked.

"We made sure she hadn't fallen in the water, which is just a few inches deep. But we knew she hadn't gone far. Her buddy saw her just before we did the body count. Mrs. Keefer, the camp director, told us not to pay much attention to Stephanie's disappearances because then she might stop doing them. So we were supposed to pause and wait fifteen minutes before starting a search. We'd tried everything else to make her stop taking off."

"So you and Casey know the Willow Trail well?"

"Every root, every tree, every branch, pretty much."

"Casey searched that particular trail many times after Stephanie's final disappearance, isn't that right?"

"Sure she did," I said. "Casey thought Stephanie might have wandered back to the camp that way from the sleep-out, since that's the trail we followed to get there. She searched as hard as she could. It was raining heavily that day; the rain soaked right through her rain gear, but she stayed out anyway." It felt good to be defending my friend.

"You had to leave the sleep-out in the middle of the night to rush one of the children, Deanna Brown, to the hospital, and when you returned the next morning, you asked Casey a very strange question."

I knew what Detective Bowen was getting at. "It was just a joke, a dumb joke."

Detective Bowen continued. "The search for Stephanie was well under way by that point. The senior campers had been organized into search squads, searching other trails, under Casey's direction. A counselor from another cabin had been assigned to look after the kids in your cabin, to free you and Casey up for the search. When you walked into the clearing where the sleep-out had taken place, Casey had just returned from another search of the Willow Trail. You went up to her and said, 'So, you've finally killed her, eh?' Casey's reply to that was, 'And I stuffed her body in a hollow tree.'"

I could hear my parents gasp. I couldn't look at them, so I stared back at the detective.

"It was a joke," I insisted. "We were tired and fed up with Stephanie. And we were friends—we could say stuff like that to each other. It was a dumb joke!"

"A joke?" Detective Bowen rose to her feet and

leaned over the table, staring down at me. "Then how do you explain the fact that Stephanie's body was found two days later, stuffed into a hollow tree? And how do you explain the fact that this hollow tree was located not twenty feet from the Willow Trail, the same trail Casey had supposedly searched, over and over again?"

"Detective, are you making an accusation?" Mr. Grey asked.

"I think Jessica knows more than she is letting on," Detective Bowen answered. "You can't protect her," she added, turning to me. "You can't rescue her. If she killed that little girl, she is going to prison. And you have to help us. As a human being, you have no choice. We have a dead child on our hands. Now, how is it possible that Casey searched that trail over and over and missed looking in that hollow tree?"

"We thought we were looking for a living kid who was hiding, not a dead kid stuffed into a tree!" I yelled. "We thought she was alive!"

SIX

The lawyer put a stop to the questions and got us all out of the room, through the hallway, then out the front door and back into the bright sunlight.

"You have nothing to worry about," he said to me. "Talk to the police again, if you want to, but you don't have to. I didn't like the tone of that detective," he said to my father, just before confirming their regular Wednesday morning eighteen holes at Piney Lakes Golf Club. Then he got into his car and drove away. My father got into his car. I looked around for my mother, but she was already walking away down the street. We all went in our separate directions.

I could have caught up with Mom and gone home with her, but I certainly didn't want to do that. I couldn't go to Casey's. I didn't know what to do with myself.

Then I remembered that the fair was on. I wasn't in a fair-going mood, but at least it was something to do. I unlocked my bike and headed over to the fairgrounds.

The Galloway Fall Fair was always set up in Lion's Park, an open space next to the cemetery, just in case one of the fairgoers should keel over from the excitement. It wasn't much of a fair, but Galloway's not much of a town.

I handed over a few bucks at the entrance gate, found a place for my bike, and started walking around.

Casey and I had always gone to the fair together, ever since we were small and fairs were a big deal. It was always the same—two steps and you've seen it all. Three or four kiddie rides, the same number of bigger rides, a few games of chance, booths of junk food. The prizes hardly changed from year to year. Even the baked goods and vegetables in the agricultural building looked the same.

I walked around, not really looking at anything. Several times I thought I saw Casey—once by the fishpond operated by the Lady Lions and another time by the snow-cone trailer. But of course it wasn't her.

I kept hearing her name, though.

"They arrested that Casey White."

"Charged her with murder."

"Kids today. There's something wrong with them. I

mean, we used to get away with murder, but we never *killed* anybody."

"Other children have disappeared not far from Galloway, you know. I'm not saying I have proof she was involved, but they say these people don't stop at one."

Stephanie Glass's murder was the biggest event Galloway had experienced since the building of the new gas station two years before. Maybe it was my imagination, but people seemed to clutch the hands of their children a little bit tighter and were a little quicker to panic when their child slipped out of sight for a moment.

I stood by the kiddie boat ride, watching the little kids go round and round, trailing their little fingers in the water.

August 23

Day 2

"You're not canoeing with the rest of the group this morning," Casey tells Stephanie.

The other campers are bug-walking ahead to breakfast, while Casey and I hang back to deal with Stephanie.

"Disappearing on us, especially the way you

did yesterday after swim time, was very wrong. We thought you had drowned! We were about to call the police!"

"You would have looked pretty stupid, calling the police when I wasn't drowned," Stephanie says. "They don't like it when you make false reports."

"I'm glad you know that," Casey tells her, her voice still patient and calm. "Do you know what it means to reinforce a message?"

Stephanie knows. "You tell a dog to sit, then you hit him until he does. Doesn't work with my dog. I probably don't hit him hard enough."

Casey and I glance at each other over Stephanie's head. Casey's face isn't so calm anymore.

"You should never hit anything," Casey says. "To reinforce the message that you shouldn't run away and hide, you're going to sit out this morning's canoe lesson. You can sit with the group and take part in the safety talk on shore, but you and I will sit on a bench and watch the others take the canoes out into the water."

Stephanie doesn't say anything.

"I know you think we're being mean," Casey says, "but while we are on the bench, maybe we can talk about your favorite things to do, and maybe we can do some of them at camp this week."

Stephanie turns her head, looks up at Casey and says, "You don't know anything."

I can see Casey start to respond. I try to catch her eye so I can signal to her not to bother, but she opens her mouth and keeps talking, not even caring that I might have an opinion about whether or not she should speak.

I leave her to it and race the other kids up the hill to breakfast.

I don't care about the race and I don't care about breakfast. Breakfast is just a sign that another damned day is about to begin.

Midmorning comes and we all trot over to the beach. The lifeguard leads everyone through the safety talk then has kids pair up on logs to learn how to hold a paddle.

Casey and I are busy—some of the kids can't tell their left hand from their right. We don't notice that Stephanie has slipped away from the group, gone to the dock and untied all the canoes, pushing them out into the water. The breeze blows them to the weedy part of the cove. Casey and I have to swim out after them, hauling them back to the dock one-by-one and using up all of the group's canoe time.

"I didn't do anything!" Stephanie claims when I accuse her. "Did you see me? No. So I didn't do it."

But she laughs as she watches Casey and me pull leeches off our legs. She tosses her long curly hair when the other campers moan about their lost opportunity.

"No place is safe anymore," I heard a woman nearby say as she waved back at her kid in one of the boats.

"Casey used to babysit for us," another woman said. "Never again. I'm going to take my kids to a therapist, have them checked out."

"Did she give any signs?"

"Do you think I would have left my kids with her if she had? Is that what you think?"

"I mean, now that you think back on it. Was there anything that seemed strange about her?"

"Not that you could put your finger on. She was a perfect babysitter. Always on time, always reliable, left the house tidy, the kids liked her. I never had to worry about her having boys over when we weren't there. You know, there's something strange about anyone *that* perfect. She must have been covering up for something. Drugs, most likely. Doesn't it always come down to drugs?"

My mother would have jumped down her throat. I just walked away.

I wandered over toward the sheep display, but was stopped before I got there.

"Pretty awful about Casey."

Amber Bradley was standing by my elbow. We weren't friends but we weren't enemies, either. I'd worked on a geography project with her in the sixth grade, an Incan model of some sort. She was part of the cool crowd.

"Yeah," I replied. "She's missing all the excitement."

Making derogatory remarks about the fall fair is part of the Galloway youth tradition.

"It's like those boys who shot up that school,"

Amber continued.

"Which boys, which school? And how is this like that?"

"If that little kid had carried a gun, she'd still be alive." This came from Nathan Ivory, a guy with a permanent smirk whose parents owned the stationary store in town. He was the kid Casey had body-slammed for killing her praying mantis. He and several others, all part of the gang Amber hung out with, had sauntered over to us.

The thought of horrid little Stephanie with a gun sent chills down my spine, but I didn't say that. What I said instead was, "Stephanie was eight."

"You can't start them too young," Nathan said, and then he pretended to hold a machine gun and shoot it at people. He always looked like he was auditioning for a play when he was around Amber.

"About those boys," Amber continued, tossing her hair. "Everyone said they were so normal."

"No one said that," I replied.

"You couldn't say Casey was normal."

"What do you mean by that?" I demanded.

"Oh, come on, Jess. I know she's your best friend, but even you have to admit she's weird. All that talk about bugs. You can't say good morning to her without hearing about some bug."

"She's going to be an entomologist," I reminded them.

"I'm going to be a surgeon, but I don't talk about body parts all the time," Amber said.

I had to laugh at that one. Amber didn't have the brains to pass the first-aid section of the babysitting course we took together in the eighth grade.

"I don't know if Casey has ever been on a date," one of them said. "That's weird. It's not like she's ugly or anything."

"It would fit," Nathan said. "The papers said some of Stephanie's clothing was missing. Casey must be some twisted sort of pervert."

"What?" I exclaimed, my mouth dropping open.

"Is she a perve, Jess?" Amber asked. "Because, you know, if anyone would know, it would be you, since you're so close and all."

"Yeah, you're sorta like best buddies," added Nathan.

I opened and closed my mouth like a fish out of water then turned on my heels and walked away.

"When's the last time you had a date, Jess?" one of the kids yelled after me. Their laughter followed me out of the park. So, I'm sure, did every pair of eyes at the fair.

That night, I woke up again at two a.m. I took my bike out and rode around the sleeping town. I stayed away from the police station. Instead, I rode over to Lion's Park where the fair was halfway torn down.

Underneath the dinosaur bones of the partially dis-
mantled Wild Mouse ride, I got off my bike. Because
I missed my friend, and because I hated to be left all
alone, I sat down and cried.

I ended up falling asleep under the Wild Mouse. I woke
up covered in dew and shivering in the early morning
air. I remembered that it was the first day of school.

My whole head felt thick. *I can't do this without
Casey,* I thought.

And I wasn't going to.

I pedaled home through thick fog. I didn't even
bother to shower or change. I got Mom's car keys off
the kitchen counter, unlocked the trunk of her car, and
started loading up my camping equipment. Then I went
into my bedroom and shoved clothes into my duffel
bag. Casey and I were the same size — she was a little
taller, but not much.

As I tied the bag shut I heard waking-up noises from
my parents' bedrooms, so I hurried. I scribbled a note
to Mom that I had her car, put the note on the kitchen
table, and left the house.

Casey's first court appearance was scheduled for
that morning. I wasn't able to rescue her from the police
station, with all those cops around; maybe I could rescue her from the courthouse. If I could get there early

enough to get a seat in the front of the courtroom, I'd grab Casey as soon as she was brought in. The element of surprise, that's what we needed. We'd be out of that courtroom and on the road before anybody could react. We'd disappear, camp, get jobs, lead new lives. We might even slip across the border someplace where it wasn't guarded too well. I wanted to get her as far away from Galloway as possible. And I didn't want to be there anymore either.

I was still half asleep.

The parking lot behind the courthouse was empty when I pulled in. I chose a spot that would make it easy for us to get away, and faced the car toward the highway. I turned off the motor, stretched out as much as I could behind the steering wheel and closed my eyes, just for a moment.

When I opened them again, the parking lot was full.

I was disoriented; for a second I forgot why I was there. But I pulled myself together and headed toward the courthouse door.

I could hear the crowd from the parking lot, and I saw them as soon as I rounded the corner by the entrance. Some of them carried signs: An Eye for an Eye, Justice for Stephanie—with a drawing of a noose on it. There were variations, but they were all calling for my best friend's blood.

The media was there, too. I counted television cameras from four different stations. They seemed to be interviewing people at random. Some of the people talking into the mikes had no connection to Casey or, as far as I knew, to Stephanie.

Amber Bradley was there, talking into a TV camera, groomed as if she was about to step on the runway.

"We always thought she would do something like this," Amber said, shaking her head to make her hair bounce around her shoulders. "None of us were really friends with her. She was just too weird."

I walked past Amber and went into the courthouse.

It was easy to find the right courtroom. I just followed the noise.

Another crowd was gathered outside the courtroom door.

"Why can't we go in?" someone demanded. "We have a right to go in."

Detective Bowen was there, guarding the door. "The courtroom is full," she said.

I pushed my way through the crowd. After what she'd put me through, twice, I figured she owed me a favor.

"Can I go in?" I asked her.

She didn't answer. She just let me in through the narrow opening she made in the door. I left the noise out in the hall and entered the quiet of the small courtroom.

I squished into a bench at the back, at the end of a row of people I didn't know. A few rows ahead, I recognized some people from our church. Casey's mother and father were right up front. I should have gone up to say hello but I didn't. I stared at the picture of the queen on the wall behind the judge's seat and kept my arms folded across my chest.

The judge came in and we all stood up, then we all sat down again. Then it seemed like the chief activity of the court was the shuffling and passing of papers from one person to another. For the longest time, the two lawyers up front couldn't find a piece of information—each insisted the other had it. The judge didn't change his expression. He sat and looked bored until everything was straightened out.

"Is the Crown counsel ready?" the judge finally asked.

"Yes, Your Honor," answered a tall, thin man in a well-pressed suit. "May we have Casey White brought forward, please?"

The court clerk stuck her head through a door behind the judge's bench and called out, "Casey White!"

Casey was escorted into the courtroom by two police officers. I gasped at the sight of her. I could feel my heart thumping.

Casey's long red hair hung down over her face. Her hands were shackled to a chain around her waist. Her feet were chained, too, judging by the way she shuffled. At the edge of the prisoner's box, she was turned to face her escorts. The clicks and rattles of the handcuffs and chains being removed rang through the silent courtroom. She stepped into the prisoner's box.

Casey, her hands free, pulled her hair back from her face. I gasped again. Her mother gave a little cry. Casey's face was covered with scratches, and one of her eyes was puffy and turning black.

"Your Honor, what is the meaning of this?" The defense attorney sprang to her feet. "My client was taken into custody only two days ago, uninjured. We demand to know how this happened."

"Your Honor, I'd be happy to explain," the Crown counsel offered.

"Explanations can wait until after introductions," the judge said. "Mr. Jack Tesler, I know you are here representing the Crown. Would the attorney for the defense please introduce herself to the court?"

"My name is Mela Cross. I have been retained to represent Casey White."

"Very well," the judge said. "Now, Mr. Tesler, please explain."

"The accused attempted to escape police custody and officers had to use lawful force to restrain her."

"There are video cameras all over that police station," Mela Cross said. "Could the Crown attorney produce videotaped evidence of this lawful force?"

"Unfortunately, the video camera covering the area was malfunctioning that day," Mr. Tesler answered.

"What a coincidence," Ms. Cross said, without a hint of surprise in her voice.

"There are enough emotions being displayed outside the courtroom," the judge said. "Let us try to let reason prevail in here. Ms. Cross, if your client is alleging police brutality, there are avenues for dealing with that. Mr. Tesler, if you want to add an escape custody charge to the docket, you know how to do that. If there are any further injuries to the defendant, there had better be clear tapes—and I want to see them, understood? We are here today to hear a plea and to hear arguments for and against bail. Ms. Cross, would your client like the charges read?"

"Those charges are completely ridiculous and yes, we would like them read."

"Save the speeches, Ms. Cross. The clerk of the court will now read the charges."

The clerk stood and read in a clear but expressionless voice, as if she were reading out a grocery list. Her words had nothing to do with my friend.

"That one Casey Anne White, on or about the twenty-ninth day of August, 2010, in the municipality of Galloway, unlawfully did intentionally kill Stephanie Glass and did thereby commit murder in the first degree."

"Ms. Cross, does your client wish to enter a plea at this time?"

Ms. Cross turned to Casey. In a loud, clear voice, Casey said, "Not guilty."

"Mr. Tesler, what is the Crown's position on bail?"

"Due to the serious nature of the charges, and because the accused has already proven herself to be a considerable flight risk..."

He went on and on about how dangerous Casey was.

As he talked, Casey looked around the courtroom. I knew she was looking for me. First she smiled at her parents, trying to tell them she was all right. Then she looked at me. Our eyes locked, and for a second I felt my old strength coming back. She grinned at me, then, and snapped her finger and thumb together. She was Praying Mantis, snapping the head of the prosecuting attorney.

Everyone in the courtroom followed her gaze—the judge, the lawyers, the clerks, everyone. I could see them looking at me.

I should have smiled back. I should have grinned and waved and copied her hand signal. What would it have cost me? Nothing. But I didn't do that.

What I did instead was look away. I pretended she was looking at someone else.

Bail was denied.

Casey was chained up again. I could hear the chains locked around her. I knew she'd be looking at me. I did not look up. I wasn't watching when they took her away.

I forgot that I was supposed to be rescuing her until I was back outside the courthouse again. I drove Mom's car home, put away my camping gear and took my bike to school. It was the first day of classes, but I wasn't the only one who was late.

On the television news that night the Crown prosecutor talked about Casey grinning in court. Her grin had come while he was calling her a cold-blooded killer. It did not make her look good.

SEVEN

The other kids at school gave me a wide berth for the next few days. I felt their eyes on me, though, and there would be sudden silences when I passed by groups huddled together in the hallway, classroom, or cafeteria. It seemed like they were waiting to see what I would do next. I guess I was waiting, too.

In the meantime, school life folded around me like a shroud. Before long, it was as if the summer had never happened, as if my entire life had been spent going up and down the halls of Galloway District High.

My course load was heavy. I was on an academic track for university, since I told everyone who asked that I wanted to be a gym teacher, even though I doubt I ever wanted to be anything less in my life. When I wasn't in class, I was in the cafeteria, working the cash register in return for a free meal and a few bucks a week.

Training for the cross-country team started up, and my after-school time got filled up, too. Evenings were for chores and homework.

But no matter how full I made my days, there were always gaps that Casey used to fill.

It wasn't that we'd hung out together all that much at school. She would have been busy, too, helping out the biology teacher and prepping for science fairs or competitions. But she'd always come looking for me if we didn't bump into each other between classes. Always.

Sometimes I'd test her. I would avoid all the places where we usually met, just to see if she really was interested in talking to me. If she didn't find me for a couple of days, she'd call me at home or drop by my house to see if I was sick or something. I liked that I could make her do that.

She never caught on that I was playing with her. She'd say, "Oh, there you are!" and launch into a story about whatever happened that day.

She always just seemed glad to see me.

I wonder now if that's because my absences didn't matter to her. I know she was *my* best friend. But was I hers? You can be glad to see your favorite flavor of ice cream in the freezer, but if it's not there, you can be just as happy with something else.

I wonder if that was it.

Maybe she didn't get mad at me because I just wasn't that important to her.

August 24

Day 3

That afternoon, Stephanie disappears again.

Our cabin challenges the nine-year-olds in Cabin Five to a softball game. When the time comes to head to the ball field, Stephanie cannot be found.

But I know where she is.

She is hiding behind the rolled-up volleyball nets in the back of the equipment shed. She sees that I've spotted her.

"Go ahead," I tell Casey quietly. "Don't keep Cabin Five waiting." I watch them bug-walk down the path to the ball diamond.

I close the door of the equipment shed and sit down on the top step with my back against the door. I enjoy the sun and a rare few moments to myself.

A bit of time goes by and I start hearing noises inside the shed. The door bumps against my back. I let it bump. I look up at the window and see Stephanie's pretty little face squished against the glass, staring down at me.

I can almost hear what she's thinking. Should I yell for help? Will that get me into more trouble or less?

Maybe she's just curious about what I will do next.

She bumps the door against my back a few more times.

"Let me out," she orders, but quietly.

I stay where I am.

"Let me out!" she says again, more forcefully.

"When I'm ready," I say.

"I'm telling," she says. "You're locking me in here."

"You think they'll believe you?"

Silence for a moment. Then, "You're being mean to me."

"So what?" I ask, stretching in the sun like a cat. "I don't care about you. Get lost and stay lost if you want to. You're not bothering me."

"I'll scream."

"Go ahead," I say. "They're all at softball."

She stops talking then, and I almost forget about her. It's so nice to have some no-kid time in the middle of the day.

I can't leave her in there too long because the softball game won't last forever. But I don't need to hurry, either.

After ten minutes, Stephanie starts to whine.

"It's hot in here. I'm going to faint if you don't let me out."

"Go ahead," I say.

I leave her in there for another five minutes, and then I stand up and step away from the door. I start walking toward the baseball field. Behind me I hear the door open up. I hear her step down into the path, moan in a silly, dramatic way, and fall to the ground. I don't turn around. After a moment, I hear her get up again. By the time we get to the ball game, she is running ahead of me.

Casey sees us coming and waves. I snap my finger and thumb together. She grins, nods, and makes the signal back.

For the rest of the day Stephanie stays out of my way. She doesn't disappear, and she doesn't tell anyone I kept her in the shed. I've solved the problem and I feel proud of myself. I'm better at this than Casey is. I start to daydream about a career as a child psychiatrist or even running my very own prison for children, where horrible children will turn into model citizens. I'll get medals and write-ups in national magazines.

I wake up suddenly. It's the middle of the night. Stephanie is standing by my bunk, staring down at me.

"You'll pay for what you did," she says.

Then she goes back to her own bed.

I don't sleep for the rest of the night.

Casey's first letter was waiting on the hall table when I got home from school that Friday.

I held it in my hand, turning it over and over. I kept seeing her looking at me in the courtroom and me not returning her gaze. I was afraid of what her letter would say. I folded it in half and stuck it in my back pocket.

That night I woke up just as the display on the clock radio changed to two a.m. It had been like this every night since Casey's arrest. Wake up at two, creep out of the house, ride around until I exhaust myself and can sleep again. That night I found myself riding out to Ten Willows, Casey's letter still in the back pocket of my jeans. I could feel the lump against the bicycle seat.

The back roads to the camp were almost pitch-black in the new moonlight, and the battery on my bike light gave out before I was a quarter mile from home. I navigated more by instinct than by sight.

Ten Willows Camp has winter quarters up top, near the highway. The summer camp is down below, and to get to it by road you have to go down a steep hill with an abrupt curve at the bottom. When I was younger, I used to tie a towel around my shoulders and feel it rippling behind me like a cape as I flew down the hill on my bike, Casey close by. Nervous car drivers and bicycle cowards could apply their brakes. Not Casey and me. We knew just when to turn our handlebars, just how to lean into the curve. The momentum we gathered going down the hill would shoot us through the length of the field, almost to the dining hall.

On this night, the overhanging trees made the dirt road ahead look even darker. I didn't pause at the top of the hill, like Casey and I usually did. I kept on pedaling all the way down, even when the pedals went almost too fast for my legs to keep up with them. I pedaled into an abyss—a pit of blackness that, for all I could see, could have been the end of the world. I wanted the blackness to swallow me up, to take me from this town, from the confusion in my head.

What happened instead was that I misjudged the turn and went flying into the dirt and pebbles of the road. It was a stupid accident. Fate did not even have the grace to let me pass out. I felt hurt and scared, and despite the fact that no one was around to see, embarrassed.

Nothing was broken, but my face stung from the gravel burn. I groped around for my bicycle and it, too, seemed miraculously undamaged—although I was sure the light of the day would show ravages to each of us. I decided I didn't care, got back on my bike, and rode into the camp.

I dismounted outside the long row of cabins and leaned my bike against Cabin Three, my home that last week of camp. I tried the door but of course it was locked.

I walked over to the dining hall, limping a little from my wipeout. On the other side of the hall, ten willow trees grew in a circle, majestic in their old age, with leaves that hung so plentiful and low, entering the circle was like entering a room through a beaded curtain. You have to part the branches with your hands to move through them—or you can close your eyes and walk straight into them, feeling them brush over your face like long strings of feathers.

Inside the circle sit stone benches, also in a circle. They face a little flower garden. I couldn't see them in the darkness, but I knew the pansies were still blooming and the marigolds were still golden.

In the center of the flowers is a large piece of driftwood, hauled up from the river on the camp's edge. It is so gnarly it looks like it's made of rope. There's a plaque on it with a bit of Psalm 137 carved into it:

> *On the willows, we hung up our lyres*
> *For our captors demanded songs,*
> *And our tormenters, mirth.*

After seeing it there for so many years, I could recite it by heart, like my address or my locker combination.

I could recite it but I didn't understand it, and I didn't really care what it meant.

I sat on a bench for a long while, listening to the willow trees whisper to each other. I sat there until the sweat on my body felt icy and my legs started to cramp in the chill night air. To warm up I did a slow jog back to Cabin Three. I got on my bike and headed home.

The hill was not as dark as it had been, and I realized dawn was about to break. I had to pedal fast to get home before Mom woke up. I only just made it.

I'd forgotten about my face. At breakfast Mom asked me about the cuts and scrapes. I told her I went out for an early morning run and slipped in some gravel. She told me she was glad I was working hard, then ruined it by asking why I couldn't do that all the time. I snarled at her, she snarled back, and we ended up yelling at each other.

There was only one good thing about that day. When I went to the washroom between classes, I looked at myself in the mirror. My face was scarred the way Casey's was. We looked alike now. Strangely, it made me feel better.

EIGHT

August 25

Day 4

The chaos begins.

Everything is fine to start with. Stephanie is in her bunk for the wake-up song. She stays with us for breakfast and keeps her mouth shut during Bible study.

But when we go out to the clothesline behind the cabin to get our bathing suits for morning swim, all our suits are gone.

Stephanie's is the only one hanging there.

"She's mean but she's not too bright," I say to Casey. "No swimming for her today! She's not swimming for the rest of camp."

I start to head across the cabin to where Stephanie has already changed into another bathing suit, but Casey puts her hand on my arm to stop me.

"It's underwear day!" she calls out, all chipper. "Today everyone swims in their t-shirts and underwear."

And just like that, the other campers stop complaining. They act like swimming in underwear is the most fun thing they've ever done. They chatter and screech and laugh at the way their t-shirts balloon up in the water.

I take some pleasure in seeing how annoyed Stephanie looks at being ignored, but that pleasure goes away when Casey draws her into the group and encourages her to play with the others. She ends up having a good time after all.

And I have to swim in my underwear.

Cabin Six finds our bathing suits when they're out on a nature walk. The suits are in the marsh, floating on water lilies and snagged on cattails.

"This is a bad kid," I say to Casey. "You're not

seeing her for who she really is. We've got to
make a plan to handle her or she'll ruin camp
for everyone."

"She was with us all day," Casey says. "She
must have snuck out of the cabin early in the
morning, gathered the suits off the line, and taken
them to the marsh. But I've been awake since
five-thirty. She was in her bunk the whole time."

Casey wakes up early to work on the
correspondence courses she's taking over the
summer so she can take four months off to go
to Australia.

"It must have been dark when she did it,"
Casey says. "Stephanie's actually a pretty brave
little kid."

"Brave like Jack the Ripper," I mutter, but
Casey doesn't hear me. She turns the whole
thing into a marshland lesson, helping the girls
wade through the marsh, identifying each plant a
bathing suit has landed on, pointing out the pond
skippers and the shells of dragonfly larvae

that have shed their skins.

The kids all have a great time.

Even Stephanie.

"Can I wear your hair clip?" she asks Casey in a sweet voice.

Casey doesn't much care about her clothes. But she does care about her hair clip. Her father made it for her when he was in rehab after his accident. There's a drawing of a praying mantis tooled into it.

But before Casey can tell her no, Stephanie's hand has gone up to the clip. She starts to pull.

Casey yanks her head back but Stephanie keeps a strong grip on the hair clip and yanks it away. Some of Casey's hair comes out along with it.

"Owww!" Casey cries. "That hurts! Is that a kind way to behave?" She tries to grab the hair clip back, but Stephanie runs off with it, laughing.

I chase after her. I'm a runner and she's a laughing little kid without a plan. I catch up to her easily and pry the hair clip out of her hand. She doesn't really fight me for it. But she stares at me, hard, as I hand it back to Casey.

Stephanie has finally targeted Casey.

And Casey at last begins to realize that I am right.

I opened Casey's letter during history class the next day while Mr. Cloutier was droning on and on about the history of trade unions. Inside the envelope was one sheet of paper. *Foxfire Youth Detention Center* was printed at the top of it.

I know every word of her letters by heart. They are seared in my brain. This one read:

Dear Dragonfly,

Who could have imagined that the summer would end like this? I wish I could take back every angry word I ever said to Stephanie, every time I lost my temper. I feel so bad. I feel so guilty. I'm really the one responsible for her death.

I hate it here. They won't let me go outside. I get

strip-searched every time they move me from one place to another. You'd think that wouldn't be a big deal, after a whole summer of getting changed in front of campers. But it does bother me.

They keep me in a cell all by myself, away from the other girls. They say I'm a security risk because of my so-called escape attempt from the police station. I didn't try to escape, you know. They left me sitting on a bench beside an open door. I saw some grasshoppers leaping around in the weeds so I walked outside to get a closer look. Being under arrest didn't seem real to me until six big cops landed on top of me and ground my face into the sidewalk.

My family is taking this really hard. They say your parents and other people in town are being kind to them, but I know they are lying, although not about your parents. I saw the faces of the people in that courtroom. They'd like to hang me from the Welcome to Galloway sign. I can't say I'd disagree with them.

I'm allowed only one piece of paper and I'm running out of room. Come on, Dragonfly, swoop on over here and rescue me. Turn the world back to the night of the sleep-out, when Stephanie was still alive and we were just annoyed with her.

With love from your faithful sidekick,
Praying Mantis

I read through the letter over and over, ignoring the history lecture and almost missing the bell at the end of class. I tried to imagine Casey in a cell. I got an image in my head of her locked inside one of her own killing jars.

In my next class, English Lit, I turned to an empty page in my loose-leaf binder. I wrote at the top of the page: *Dear Praying Mantis*. I stared at that for a while, scribbled over it, and wrote, *Dear Casey* in its place.

I scribbled through that, too.

All weekend long, I planned to answer her letter. Homework and chores got in the way. Mom got me a weekend job making beds in the nursing home where she worked. I changed dozens of peed-on sheets, told the old people it didn't matter, and rejoiced when I got out of there.

There were lots of excuses for not answering her

letter, all very good ones.

Late that night, I biked down to Casey's street and rode around and around in a circle in front of her house.

"Jess?"

I was so startled I nearly fell off my bike. Mrs. White was standing on the edge of her lawn. She was in her bathrobe. Her face looked hollowed-out and her back was stooped. It looked like she was holding herself together with toothpicks.

I got off my bike. "I'm sorry if I woke you up. I didn't think I was making any noise."

"You weren't," she said. "I just haven't been able to sleep much. You either, by the looks of it."

"No," I admitted. "Not much." I stared at the ground below my handlebars. I didn't want to look at Mrs. White.

"Come inside," she said. "I'll make some cocoa. Maybe it will make us both sleepy."

I wanted to go in with her. I wanted to sit in her calm and clean kitchen and drink hot chocolate, then sit in the bug den with her and Mr. White and watch an old black and white movie from their collection.

"I should go home," I said instead.

"What happened that night?" she whispered.

I didn't answer her. I think she was asking the universe more than she was asking me.

"Why are they blaming Casey? They know her. She grew up here. They know us. What happened that night?"

"I should go home," I said again.

Mrs. White reached over the handlebars and gave me a loving, tender hug. It was comforting and familiar, the same hug she had been giving me all my life—the same safe harbor I'd always sailed into when the storms blew inside my mother. I watched her head back across the lawn and slip inside the house. She closed the door and I was shut out.

I biked around Galloway for a while longer and ended up at the bridge. I stood and watched the river flow below me for a long time before I felt tired enough to go back home to bed.

A few days later, I leafed through my history textbook, looking for Casey's letter, where I thought I'd left it. The letter wasn't in the book. It had to be in my locker at school.

I thought no more about it until the next morning. The city newspaper had a box in front of our high school. Casey's hand-written note—printed just as she wrote it and framed in a thick black band—showed clearly through the glass of the newspaper box. I stared at it and could feel myself turning to stone.

It wasn't hard to figure out what had happened. The

letter had fallen out of my history book, and whoever had picked it up decided to turn it into a bit of quick cash—or some other advantage.

I looked into the face of every kid heading into the school building. Any one of them could have done it.

And then I stopped looking, because suddenly I didn't want to know who'd done it. Because if I knew for sure, I'd have to do something.

Why would someone betray *me*? What had I ever done to anybody?

What if Casey thought *I'd* given the letter to the newspaper? Now I'd have to write to her and tell her it wasn't me.

And then I was angry at Casey. Why would she think I had done it? Where was her sense of loyalty?

"Good morning, Dragonfly," giggled some girls, bumping into me as they passed by.

Something special, something private, which had remained a secret between us all these years, was now out in the open for the world to see and laugh at.

I leaned against the newspaper box and vomited all over it.

NINE

"What is this?"

Mom confronted me at dinner that night. "How did this happen?" She slammed the newspaper down so hard she knocked over my glass of milk.

I got up to get a cloth.

"Leave it!" she shrieked. "Answer me!"

"Her letter must have slipped out of my history book," I said.

Dad was working late. There was nobody to buffer her.

"You let her letter get away from you? And now look what's happened!"

"I didn't plan it," I protested.

"But you don't seem very upset about it, either. Why aren't you angry? Why aren't you upset? Why aren't you railing?"

"You don't know what I'm feeling," I shot back at her. "Besides, you're railing enough for the both of us."

"Is this whole town *crazy*?" Mom threw up her hands and strode about the dining room with dizzying speed. She grabbed the phone and punched in a number. "Gerald, I want you to sue that newspaper! I want you to find out who gave them that letter and have them charged with theft. Hire a detective; get the police on this. You're a lawyer, you'll know what to do. I don't care what it costs. We'll put up our house, we'll cash in our insurance—" She slammed down the receiver. "Damn answering machine."

She went into the living room. I could hear her muttering to herself. I grabbed a wet cloth from the kitchen and wiped up the milk, then cleared the table. Mom never ate when she got like this—the meal she'd prepared was inedible anyway. The potatoes were still raw and the meatloaf barely had a brown tinge to it. I put the food back in the oven to cook properly and made a peanut butter and banana sandwich to take to my room.

Gerald Grey had received calls like that before. He knew better than to act on them. I'd seen Mom go off so many times that it didn't worry me anymore. Not really. I knew she'd get only just so crazy, then my dad would call the doctor, and the ambulance would come. She'd spend a few weeks in the mental health ward of the city hospital, get zapped with electricity, and have her meds adjusted. Then they'd return her to us—a little shaky, a little forgetful, a little embarrassed, but otherwise all right.

Dad and I had learned to live with it. One year, after Mom went through the savings account in three months and ran up huge debts on the credit cards, he limited her access to their money, so there wasn't too much damage she could do.

Whenever she started feeling better, she'd go off her meds. She'd get great schemes in her head—landscaping the yard, or getting herself into medical school, or painting the shingles on the roof white to attract better vibes from the universe. Sometimes she made speeches on street corners. The town knew her and tolerated her. That's something good you can say about Galloway. No one ever made fun of my mom. Not even other kids. That's because their parents are probably even stranger than mine.

If someone's parents are a *little* weird—for example if they wear checkered pants and striped shirts at the same time—they're fair game. But if something is seriously strange, no one says anything. When my mom went crazy, or another kid's mom went bald from chemotherapy, or Bruce Catskill's dad beat him with a big jug of orange juice in the parking lot of the grocery store in front of Bruce's friends, no one laughed. It's like kids know that's a heavy thing, that's off-limits.

Dad reacted to Mom's condition by becoming so steady to the point of being boring. Over the years, he grew more and more even-tempered. If he were a pencil line, he'd be gray lead, straight across the page, no ups or downs. Mom would be brilliant colors in squiggles and circles, filling up all the blank spaces—and then deep black, running low along the bottom.

"What if I turn out like my mom?" I used to ask Casey. "What if I turn out like my dad?"

"What if you wake up one morning and you're a giant cockroach?" Casey would answer.

That answer always gave me great comfort. Some things you can control, some things you can't. For the time being, I wasn't like either of my parents and I wasn't a cockroach. I could go on with that.

When I went downstairs to turn the oven off, Mom was sitting in the dark.

"I've never had a best friend, Hey Jude," she said. I heard the chink of glass as she poured herself a drink. I caught a whiff of whiskey. Dad didn't keep liquor in the house. Mom must have brought it in and hid it from him. "I always wanted one, someone who would be as much a part of me as my breath and my skin. But I never had one. Sit down," she said, but gently. "Sometimes I pretend I've got one. Isn't that silly? A woman as old as I am, with an imaginary friend? When I'm walking around town, I pretend she's with me and we laugh at the funny things we see. Everything is funny when you've got a best friend. But you know that."

She said nothing for a long while, just kept sitting and drinking. Thinking she'd forgotten about me, I stood up to go back to my room.

"Be a friend to your friend, Jude," she said, her voice barely above a whisper. "Be a friend to your friend."

I went back upstairs to my bedroom.

I went out again that night, waking up as soon as the clock display read 2:00 a.m. I biked around the residential streets, looking at the houses, dark with people sleeping inside. Sometimes a dog would bark. Once I heard someone hollering, his words muffled by the walls of his house.

The pedals moved under my feet and I thought about people yelling at each other in the darkness, about couples lying cold next to each other in bed, distant and lonely. I thought about people crying behind closed doors and the nakedness of nighttime emotion, unprotected by the civilities of the day.

I moved like a ghost through my town.

August 26

Day 5

The campers are at pottery. Casey and I finally have some quiet time without the kids. We're in the craft hut, looking through the remains of the art supplies. I want to head down the Riverside Trail. There's a spot where we dangle our feet in the water as it bubbles around the rocks.

"Go ahead," says Casey. "Go relax. I can do this."

"I don't want to go by myself," I say. "What's the fun in that?"

She doesn't say anything. She keeps sorting through boxes and looking in cupboards.

I can just go, I think. She doesn't need me here.

"This will work," she says, holding up some packs of clear plastic painters' drop-sheets. "We can turn these into butterfly wings. What kind of paint is over there?"

"I have an idea," I say, making a show of looking through the paint. "Camp ends Thursday morning. Let's stay on a couple of days after everyone goes."

"The cabins will be locked up."

"So? We can just sleep out in the meadow."

"School starts Tuesday," she says, joining me at the paint cupboard and selecting the paint she wants. "I wanted to get my correspondence courses done before that."

"So, do them in the meadow," I say. "Come on—a night or two of camping, no little kids around, before school starts and we get busy again. After all, we don't know if we'll be back here next summer. You may fly off to study some weird bug in Bolivia or Mongolia or somewhere."

"Yeah, sure," Casey says. "Let's do it. A couple of days would be good."

She puts the paints in a shallow box, grabs some brushes, and heads out. I follow her.

"You don't sound like you want to."

"Of course I want to. It will be fun."

"For two nights or for one? One, right? You'll

put up with me for one night."

She stops. "What are you talking about? We'll have fun. I can gather up all my insect traps and we can check the trails for tuck-shop trash. It will be like we're putting the camp to bed—Is that Stephanie?"

It is. I can recognize that damned pink Tinker Bell shirt from across the camp.

She is being marched through the field by Jan, the pottery instructor.

"She's all yours," Jan says. "She's done with pottery."

"What happened?" I ask.

"She kept throwing clay at people and wrecking their projects."

"Why did you do that?" Casey asks her.

"Just for fun," Stephanie says.

"She's all yours," Jan says again, and leaves the brat with us.

"You might as well help us get ready for arts and crafts," Casey says.

"I want to look through your microscope," Stephanie says.

"You just got thrown out of pottery," I say. "Why should you get what you want?"

"Because my mother paid a lot of money to send me here so that I could do what I want to do. And I want to look through your microscope."

"Not now," Casey says. "Now we are getting ready for arts and crafts."

"No."

We don't answer her. She stops asking. We set up the picnic tables for crafts and the rest of the cabin soon joins us. Casey cuts big butterfly shapes out of the plastic drop cloths and gets the kids to paint designs on them. While the paint is drying, we go on a hunt for long sticks. Two sticks get attached to each butterfly. The kids run and swoop with them across the field, the butterflies blowing behind them, and I have to admit that they look pretty good.

Casey and I sit on the picnic table, tightening

paint lids and watching the kids run around.

"What I said before," I begin, "about you not wanting time later. I know it wasn't true. It's just that the summer has gone by so fast. Things are going to change soon. Everything has gone by so fast—"

"How many kids are out there?" Casey asks, interrupting me. "One, two, three, four—I wish they'd hold still...there's only seven butterflies." She stands up and raises the whistle to her lips to blow the buddies signal.

"Leave it," I say. "How many times are we going to chase after her? The kids are having fun. Leave them be."

"We should go look for her," Casey says. "Who knows what she's throwing in the swamp?"

"Maybe she'll be eaten by a snapping turtle," I say.

"Or a praying mantis," says Casey.

We both make our secret signal, and we laugh. Casey is back with me again. I am happy enough to suggest running with the kids, and we race out onto the field.

"We are starlings," Casey tells them, "and we are hungry for butterflies!"

We play this new game of chase until the bell rings to tell everyone to get cleaned up for supper. We bug-walk back to the cabin, sweaty and happy, to find that Stephanie has wreaked a path of destruction. All the kids' crafts—their spider webs made from sticks and wool, the dragonfly mobile hanging from the ceiling, the pictures made with stuff they found on nature hikes—are torn and crumpled on the floor.

And the microscope is missing.

"What are you looking at me for?" Stephanie says from her bunk, where she's reading a Ramona book and eating a contraband Three Musketeers bar. "I didn't do anything."

I leave Casey with the kids and go find Mrs. Keefer.

"Stephanie can't stay with us," I say. "She's

making everybody miserable. And she stole
Casey's microscope! Casey babysat for six months
to buy it."

What if there are difficult people in Australia?
Casey will ask me. How will I manage without
you? You'd better come with me.

Mrs. Keefer sighs and shakes her head in
defeat. She takes me into her little closet of
an office, pulls Stephanie's file and punches her
aunt's number into the phone. Mrs. Keefer leaves
a cautious message, asking Stephanie's aunt to
call back to discuss some issues with Stephanie's
behavior.

"You didn't make it sound very serious."

"Stephanie is eight years old," Mrs. Keefer
says. "I know she's a handful, but she's not an
axe-murderer."

"Not yet," I mumble.

"But if the two of you really can't handle her,
I'll see if Bones will keep her in the infirmary
until her aunt can come and get her. I hope I

wasn't wrong in trusting you two with a cabin. Does Casey feel the same as you?"

I haven't asked her. I didn't even tell her where I was going when I left her alone, cleaning up the mess and trying to soothe the crying, angry kids.

"Casey and I are in complete agreement," I say.

Mrs. Keefer doesn't look like she believes me, but I don't care. I don't care if she thinks I'm a bad counselor, either. I don't need this job next summer. I can get a much better job, one that pays a lot more money, doing things that are much more important than teaching clapping games and Bible verses to a bunch of kids who could care less.

I march back to the cabin in triumph and plunge into the cleanup.

"Where have you been?" Casey asks me, actually looking annoyed with me.

"Fixing the problem," I say.

I take the broom and start sweeping beside

Stephanie's bunk. She's still lying there, eating chocolate and watching all the activity with a twisted little smile on her face.

"Pack your bags," I say to her, quietly.

"Why?"

In reply all I do is smirk and continue sweeping.

Mrs. Keefer sidles up to me at the beginning of campfire that night.

"I talked to Mrs. Glass," she says. "She won't be returning early—to rebook the flight will cost too much money. She also says her sister isn't an option—she has her own kids and they don't get along with Stephanie. She's going to have to stay with us until Camp ends. I asked Bones about keeping Stephanie with her, but she said there are a couple of kids already in the infirmary—a poison ivy case and an intestinal bug of some kind. So, I'm afraid you will have to manage. If you think you can't, I'll send one of the older counselors to your cabin to take over from you and you can go to her cabin."

I'm not about to do that. "We'll manage," I say.

"I'll have another talk with Stephanie. And I'll check in with you as often as I can."

She heads down to the fire pit to lead in the singing of "Fire's Burning."

I hear a child's voice in my ear.

"Do you still want me to pack?"

I turn around. It's Stephanie, of course. She's been listening the whole time. She doesn't look at me. She's watching Mrs. Keefer, waiting for the camp director to point to our section, and then she joins in the round.

Fire's burning, fire's burning
Draw nearer, draw nearer
In the glowing, in the glowing
Come sing and be merry.

Her voice is sweet, she is smiling, and I wonder if anybody would miss her if I strangled her in the night and dumped her body in the river.

TEN

Stephanie's death continued to be big news.

Even though it seems to happen a lot, you know—school shootings and things—children killing children is news. I don't know why. Children can be terrorists. I think adults block that out of their memories and create instead this picture of childhood as a time of joy and innocence. They forget about being bullied, being tormented, being left out. They forget the violence on the schoolyard and in the hall between classes—body slams and kicks, and hard things flying at your head for no reason you can see.

Why do people think children can't be violent? Children are people. People are violent.

"Bugs aren't violent," Casey said one night.

We were in her den, watching the news with her folks. A man had just killed his whole family, including a neighbor's kid who was playing over at the house. Then he shot the neighbor, who had come running at the sound of gunfire, then shot bullets through the windows of the homes across the street.

"Bugs aren't violent," Casey said. "Bugs kill to eat. We kill each other for no reason at all."

That's all Casey really wanted. She just wanted people to behave as well as bugs.

Stephanie's death was particularly big news.

First, because Stephanie had been so pretty.

Second, because Casey is also attractive: not pretty but strong-looking and striking—at least I've always thought so. She was also a model teenager and had won all sorts of state and national science awards. She was the last person you'd expect to turn into a murderer. This gave the media lots of opportunities to do stories like, "What's Wrong With Our Youth?" and "Is There A Monster At Your Supper Table?"

Third, because Casey had been Stephanie's camp counselor, which led to many debates in the press and on radio phone-in shows about how society can protect its children. More surveillance was a popular solution. Spy-tech companies reported a boost in sales of devices parents could use to spy on their kids.

And last, because of the whole insect thing. It was weird, it was exotic, and it set this case apart from other kid-on-kid violence. Some idiot called the case "A small town *Silence of the Lambs*," because that story had an insect and Casey liked insects. It made no sense, but the idea caught on.

One columnist wrote about Casey's unhealthy obsession with science, that perhaps her preference for bugs over boys indicated some deep-seated perversion.

"Answer them!" Mom said to me, waving the newspaper in my face at the breakfast table. "Write them a letter. Tell them the truth. Stand up to them!"

The louder she got, the more I backed away.

And my father? His expression never changed. He ate his All Bran and never looked up.

Stephanie's funeral was the next big event in town. It had been delayed because the coroner and the police took their time releasing her body.

It was held on a Friday morning at our church. Practically the whole town was there. Stephanie's entire third-grade class was there—at least they would have been her class if she'd survived the summer. The kids laid flowers on the alter. One little girl read a poem, one of those "we will never forget you" deals. I would have found it more moving if I hadn't seen that same girl mugging for the TV cameras before the service started.

People nudged each other when Mom and I walked into the church. Within moments, the whole congregation, except for Stephanie's mother, was twisting around to look at me.

"What are you staring at?" Mom demanded. I got her into a pew before she could say anything more.

I looked for Casey's parents but I didn't see them.

Funerals are sad events, and I was of course sad that Stephanie was dead, but I found myself feeling angrier and angrier as the service went on. Everyone wanted to get in on the action. The junior choir sang. Kids in the choir whispered and giggled until the camera was pointed at them, then they instantly shut up and looked sorrowful. Reverend Fleet strutted like a peacock to the pulpit and said the benediction like he'd been practicing with a drama coach.

TV turns everything into garbage.

But that's not what was making me angry. It was Stephanie, that pain-in-the-neck kid who had gotten herself killed. She'd turned what should have been a fun last year of high school into a nightmare. Mom's illness was taking over because of her, my friend was in jail because of her. I was lonely and a social pariah.

Because of her.

As the service went on, my anger shifted away from Stephanie. She had been just a little kid, after all. She was annoying but she hadn't asked to be killed. It was silly to be angry with her.

But I was still angry, although I didn't feel the full force of it until the service was over and we were outside of the church.

Mrs. Glass, followed by all the TV cameras, came up to me.

"Why did you let her do it?" she asked me, her voice cold and clear. "You must have known all along what she was like, and still you left her alone with those girls, with my Stephanie. As far as I'm concerned, you're as guilty as she is. How could you let her do it? You knew what she was like!"

I froze. A dozen microphones were thrust into my face and the cameras zoomed in close. I could have—should have—turned and walked away. I could have—should have—said something dignified and sympathetic about Mrs. Glass's loss. What I did instead was open my stupid mouth and say, "I...I...I didn't know she was like that."

The barrage of media questions that followed my burst of idiocy jarred me out of my stupor and I backed away. The crowd thinned out then, sliding into waiting cars and limousines for the drive to the cemetery.

In that moment, my anger turned to Casey. She was to blame for this. She had left me all alone out here to deal with this madness. Even if she hadn't actually killed Stephanie, she hadn't been doing her job right. She had let Stephanie be killed. I thought back to Casey's letter. Casey was right. She was guilty.

All of this mess was Casey's fault. I warned her. If she'd listened to me, we could have put a stop to that kid, but Casey always had to do things her own way. I felt such a rage then that my body actually trembled.

I looked around for Mom. She was on the sidewalk, standing as far as possible from the line of cars now filling with mourners. Beside her were Casey's mother and father.

They had come, after all. I wondered why they hadn't gone inside during the service. They were church members. They should have been there.

Then, gripped by a sudden notion, I spun around to look at the church steps. The wheelchair ramp had been taken down.

I hated Galloway then. I hated, hated, hated my home town.

But I hated myself more, because I knew that, without Casey to lean on, I didn't have the guts to stand up to it.

August, 28 - 31

Day 6 - 9

It is all-out war now. We divide to try to conquer.

One of us takes the seven good kids and one of us stays close to Stephanie. We try to move as a group. We try not to let it show that one of us is always on Stephanie-watch, but she figures it out anyway. And she enjoys it.

I hate it. I hate being in charge of the seven good kids, because it takes too much effort to keep them entertained. And I hate being in charge of Stephanie, because that takes even more effort.

And it doesn't really work. She still manages to give us the slip. Casey is right—the kid is brave. She even crawls under the cabin to hide, where there are spiders and weeds and probably garter-snake nests.

Other counselors watch out for her, and so do the adult staff, marching her back to us when they find her off where she's not supposed to be. She gets lectures, she gets warnings. She does as she pleases. Casey's microscope turns up at the back of the mess-hall broom closet. It's smashed into pieces. Stephanie smiles and says, "Prove it."

She keeps stealing. Flashlights, hats, shoes, whatever she wants. One night she tries taking Casey's praying mantis hair clip again, crawling right up into Casey's bunk to get it while Casey is sleeping. Casey wakes up with a jolt, just in time, then Stephanie starts yelling that Casey almost made her fall off the top bunk and hurt herself. It takes a lot of work and a lot of patience to get the cabin quiet again. Kids get upset about one thing and they suddenly remember they are upset about a lot of things, and there are tears and tantrums and all kinds of chaos.

Casey and I get dirty looks from other counselors.

"If you can't control your cabin, maybe you should go work at Burger World," they say. I hate them all. I sneak into the Director's office while she's eating supper and call the aunt myself. All I get is an answering machine. I ask her to come and get her niece. But I don't hold my breath.

We talk about canceling the sleep-out. In fact, we do decide to cancel it. We have a hard enough time keeping track of Stephanie in the enclosed space of the cabin. We could not possibly control her in a dark field some distance away from the main camp.

But then, just as the last days of camp approaches, she seems to calm down. She still disappears, but not for long. She's already stolen everything she wants to. We are worn out and just want the camp to end. She decides to almost-behave.

And we decide to have the sleep-out after all.

ELEVEN

The legal machinery really cranked into action once Stephanie was buried, as if it would have been unseemly for it to do so before then.

Two lawyers visited me in one day.

First came Jack Tesler. He showed up soon after I got home from school. Mom answered the door. She hadn't said a word to me since my stupid comment to Mrs. Glass was aired on the news. I heard the lawyer identify himself and I heard her slam the door in his face. She bolted it against him and hit the door with the flat of her hand, to drive home her point. I thought about going out the back door and sneaking around to the front and talking to him in the driveway, out of embarrassment at Mom's behavior, but I stayed where I was. I didn't owe him an explanation. I didn't owe him anything.

I had a short babysitting job after supper and when I got home, Casey's lawyer was sitting in our living room. She was drinking tea from one of the good china cups. Mom had laid out an assortment of bakery squares.

"She is the most wonderful girl," Mom was saying as I walked into the room. I thought she was talking about me until she said, "I'd be proud to be a character witness for her. Oh, here's my 'Hey Jude.'"

"It's Jess," I said, shaking Mela Cross's outstretched hand.

"I've heard all about you from Casey," Mela said.

"They've been best friends since they were small," Mom said. "Jude will help you all she can."

Mela managed to smile at my mother and, at the same time, peer at me with a critical eye. "Mrs. Harris, would you mind if I took Jude out for a walk?"

"Call me Vivian," Mom said, then practically pushed me out the door.

At least the sun had gone down. I felt much more comfortable in the dark by this point. Mela seemed to know that. We chitchatted for a while as we walked, mostly about Ten Willows and how the kids at school were reacting to Casey's arrest.

"Let's have a cup of coffee," she suggested.

"I don't drink coffee," I lied.

"Hot chocolate, then. I'm buying." She steered me

into one of Galloway's many donut shops, keeping up the small talk until we were settled in a small booth. I sat across from her. The light in the donut shop was very bright.

I looked around. It was obvious that people knew who we were. When I made eye contact, they looked away, staring down at their walnut crullers or giving their coffee another stir.

"Casey's a rather remarkable young woman," Mela said, drawing my attention back to her.

"Yes, she is," I agreed. "Very smart, too."

"She has an uncanny capacity for loyalty," Mela continued, as if I hadn't spoken. "Uncanny, especially in a world where people have more loyalty to brands of toothpaste or blue jeans than they have to ideas. Or to friends."

I pretended to be absorbed in spooning hot chocolate over the little hill of phony whipping cream. I felt myself growing cold. A drop of sweat ran from under my arm down my side.

"For example, in the face of mounting evidence to the contrary, she still insists on referring to you as her best friend."

If I don't look up, I thought, *she'll go away*.

"She says that you had nothing to do with her letter appearing in the newspaper."

"I didn't!" I said, perhaps a little too forcefully. My conscience should have been clear on that point but it wasn't. And I could tell from the look on Mela's face that she didn't believe me.

I had nothing to say to that, so I said nothing.

"Tell me, Jude, has Casey done you some monumental wrong? Has she injured you in some way? Are you angry at some crime she's committed against you?"

An image came into my head then—a collage of images, really—of Casey with her head near the ground, staring at an anthill or watching a hornet walk across her hand, her whole attention absorbed. Nothing left for me.

"No," I said. "Of course not."

"Has she disappointed you? Betrayed you?"

I shook my head. "She's my best friend."

"Friendships can be complicated," Mela said. "They shouldn't be. When two people like each other, everything should be easy. But humans are good at making things hard."

I tried to think of something to say but there was no need. Mela was into a monologue.

"For example," she went on, "there's the matter of the Tinker Bell t-shirt that showed up in Casey's bag. Stephanie was the only girl in your cabin to have a t-shirt with Tinker Bell on it. Plus, it was her favorite shirt—

she got it at Disney World and it had her name on it. She wore it almost all the time, and everyone assumed she had it on when she was killed, because after they searched her bag and the cabin was cleaned, it wasn't anywhere to be found. But then they found Stephanie's body without the t-shirt. The rest of her clothes were accounted for, except for that shirt. So then everyone guessed that her killer had taken it as some kind of a trophy. The police got a warrant to search Casey's house and they found the shirt in her duffel bag. And then they arrested her and charged her with murder. Do you follow me so far?"

I kept stirring the hot chocolate.

"Casey can explain everything," Mela continued. "She says Stephanie had a nosebleed on the last day. You were with the rest of your girls at archery and she'd taken Stephanie back to the cabin because she kept trying to shoot arrows at the other kids. She says on the way back to the cabin Stephanie fell and her nose bled a little—not bad enough to go to the infirmary, just a little. But some of her blood got on the Tinker Bell t-shirt. Stephanie became hysterical. Casey offered to wash the blood out of it before it set, but Stephanie wouldn't calm down. She scratched up Casey's arms until they were bleeding. That's how both girls' blood ended up on the shirt.

"In the midst of the struggle over the shirt, Stephanie yanked the praying mantis hair clip out of Casey's hair, pulling out some strands of hair with it. She shoved the clip into her pocket and refused to give it back. Casey decided to wait until Stephanie calmed down before trying to get it back. But she never got the chance."

Mela sat back in the booth and watched me for a moment before continuing.

"You were the one to pack up Stephanie's things," Mela said. "The campers had gone and the camp director had sent you to pack up both your belongings and Casey's, and then sweep out the cabin. She says you were whining about having to take part in the search and she sent you to Cabin Three because she was tired of hearing you complain."

"That's not fair," I said.

"Shut up," Mela said, but quietly. She went on.

"You were the one to put Stephanie's things together and carry them up to the dining hall for her parents to take home. You were the one to put Casey's things together. But most of Casey's things were already together, weren't they? Other than the clothes she had taken with her on the sleep-out, every piece of clothing she had at camp was washed, dried, folded neatly, and packed into her duffel. That's what the police found when they searched her bag—her clothes ordered and nicely packed away. But shoved down into the middle of them was Stephanie's Tinker Bell shirt, rolled up in a ball.

"Casey said you must have put it in there. You said you didn't. So the police think Casey is lying about that, and lying about everything else. And you made that ridiculous, inflammatory statement to Mrs. Glass at the funeral—in front of a TV camera! What were you thinking?

"Jess, it's not too late to turn this around, you know. It's not too late to do the right thing."

The fake whipping cream was now an oily puddle at the top of the cooling chocolate. I kept playing with it.

Mela grabbed the spoon from my hand and slammed it down on the table. I knew without looking that every head in the donut shop had snapped to attention and every eye was now zoomed in on us.

"You are some piece of work," Mela said. "No emotions. Have you no soul?"

All I could manage in response was another feeble, "That's not fair."

She stared at me in silence for such a long time I started thinking about getting up to leave.

I started to rise. Mela reached across the table and grabbed my wrist.

"You think she did it, don't you?"

I met her eyes for a few seconds. Then I looked away

again and yanked my arm out of her grip.

Mela stood up. "I won't repeat any of this to Casey. She wouldn't believe me anyway. *She* knows what it means to be a friend. At least I have your mother as a witness."

"My mother is not well," I said.

"Your mother is well enough," Mela said, putting on her jacket. "Sanity looks like madness in an insane world."

With that, she walked out.

The other donut shop customers were staring openly now, clearly watching the show and not caring that they were being nosey. I looked down into my now-cold hot chocolate, wanting to give Mela time to get away. She was nowhere around when I left.

TWELVE

I didn't get any sleep at all that night.

When two a.m. rolled around, I got up and went biking as usual. This time I went out to the industrial area on the edge of town where the roads are long and straight. I pedaled like mad down one length of the road, working up a sweat, then turned around and biked slowly back the other way, letting myself cool down until I was shivering all over. Then I turned around and pedaled hard until I was overheated again. It made no sense, but it passed the time. I imagined myself conducting a scientific experiment into body temperature. I had a whole fantasy worked out in my head about receiving international recognition for my work and getting write-ups in the paper about it, bigger write-ups than Casey's. Pretty lame, I know, but that's what went on in my head.

It distracted me from having to remember the donut shop conversation with Mela Cross. Her words had made me feel small and cheap. "Have you no soul?" she'd asked.

Of course I didn't believe Casey had killed Stephanie. I could run through the so-called evidence better than her attorney could, striking down every bit of it. Why hadn't I said that?

Because if I'd said it, the next step would be that I would have to agree to testify. There would be more meetings, more questions, more people looking at me, and more battles to fight. I just wanted it all to be over.

The more the conversation ran through my head, the angrier I got. Who was this lawyer to pass judgment on me? She didn't know me! She didn't know my life. I hated her. And I was mad at Casey for sending that woman after me.

The house lights were on when I got home around four in the morning. I panicked and rode around in the street in front of the house for a while, working up enough nerve to go in. It was only the thought that Mom might have called the police to report me missing that finally prompted me to go inside.

Mom was in the kitchen. I could smell something baking as soon as I walked in the door. She didn't say anything to me about me being out. All she said was

"Wash these muffin tins for me, will you, my 'Hey Jude'?"

One batch of muffins was already on cooling trays. Mom was hunched over her recipe book, combining ingredients for another batch. I washed the tins then greased and floured them for her. Despite the warmth of the kitchen, I was beginning to shiver in my sweat-drenched clothes. I went up to my room, undressed, and buried myself under the blankets. I doubt she noticed that I'd left.

I slept a little — just dozed, really. Mom baking in the middle of the night was a bad sign. I kept jarring awake every few minutes, afraid she'd forgotten what she was doing and had set the house on fire. When my alarm clock went off at seven, I felt like I'd been at war all night. A hot shower cleaned me, but it didn't revive me.

The kitchen was sparkling clean when I went down to breakfast. Mom was putting fresh muffins in an old cookie tin she'd lined with wax paper. "Have some orange juice," she said. "Have a muffin."

Dad was at the table, his nose in the paper, a muffin sliced and buttered in front of him. He'd taken a couple of bites. I caught his eye above the newspaper and he gave a slight nod. The muffins were okay to eat.

"The muffins are fine. There's no need for your little signal," Mom said. I guiltily took two from the platter, although I had no appetite for even one. They tasted fine, but I had to drink a lot of juice to get them down.

"I'd like you to take these muffins over to the Whites' on your way to school," Mom told me, fitting the lid onto the cookie tin.

I put down my juice glass. I didn't want to go over there. I glanced at Dad for help but his whole face was buried in paper.

"I have to be at school early today," I lied. "History project."

"It will take you two minutes," Mom said. "You don't have to stay, you don't even have to go in, just knock on the door and hand over the tin."

"I don't have time!" I said again, more forcefully.

In two steps she crossed the kitchen and stood almost on top of me. "Take the tin," she ordered, holding it out to me.

I backed away from the table so fast I knocked over the chair. "I told you, I don't have time!"

"Take it!" She pushed the tin into my stomach.

I flung up my hands to avoid touching it.

Mom's glare bore holes right through me. She banged the tin down on the table, rattling the breakfast dishes.

I fled the kitchen. Dad, I'm sure, remained safely behind his paper.

I dragged myself through school that day, learning nothing, dozing off in my classes, and making mistakes in my cafeteria job. There was a quiz in Biology, but I might as well not have bothered.

"I know you are trying for an athletic scholarship, Jessica." Old Miss Burke kept me behind after class. She was the oldest teacher in the school and a good friend of Casey's. "Your academic grades have to be good, too. It's still early in the year, of course, but don't allow yourself to get into bad habits…"

She droned on and on, giving me advice that I was barely able to stay awake to hear.

"Had any more letters from Casey?" Amber and her followers cornered me after the last class when I was on my way to my locker.

"None of your business," I said.

"Oh, now, don't be like that. Casey is our friend, too, you know. You don't have a monopoly on her."

"Casey is not your friend," I replied.

"What's the matter?" someone asked. "Jealous?"

I pushed through the group and went on ahead down the hall. Nathan caught up with me.

"Hey, Jess, don't be mad," he said, taking my arm. "We were just having a bit of fun."

"At *my* expense."

"I'm sorry about that. It's just that this is the biggest thing that's ever happened in this town. It's got us all kind of rattled, you know?"

I could count on one hand the number of times Nathan had talked to me since kindergarten. He had always been one of the cool kids, even when he was little. Other cool kids would flock around him, all in the same nice clothes with nice haircuts—hair cut by professional stylists in the salon, not cut by their mothers with pinking shears the night she thought she was Edward Scissorhands.

Nathan was looking at me as if I was one of them, not a freak. I decided to accept his apology. For now, anyway.

"Come out and have a Coke or something with us," he invited, gesturing back at the others in the group who were all watching us. "We usually go to The Cactus after school and sort of unwind before going home. Why don't you come with us?"

Nathan didn't have to tell me they went to The Cactus. I'd often seen them there, always at the same table by the window, eating French fries and being easy with each other. They were an exclusive group, as exclusive as Galloway ever gets. I had certainly never been asked to join them before.

In the seconds after Nathan's invitation, a conversation I'd had with Casey last year came into my head.

"Who needs them?" she said, after I expressed longing to join the group at The Cactus. "If we were part of that group, we'd have to spend money every day after school, money it takes too long to earn. Plus, they never talk about anything."

"How would you know what they talk about?"

"I've heard them in class. They never express an original thought, never show any passion for anything, only know just enough of the material to get by. All they like to do is poke fun at people—and they're not even funny about it. What could they talk about?"

"You don't know everything," I said. "Maybe they just don't like showing off in front of the teachers." As though I could seriously accuse Casey of showing off. You have to care what people think of you before you can be a show-off.

Casey, of course, didn't take the bait. "Look, they're just kids. They're not gods. If you want to join them, march in there and plunk yourself down. Maybe I'm wrong about them and you'll have a good time. And if you don't have a good time, at least you'll know. Successful experiment either way."

I hadn't joined The Cactus gang that day or any other. I'd stuck with Casey, not because her feelings would have been hurt if I'd made other friends, but because they would not have been. She would have been fine with me doing whatever I wanted to do because she always did what she wanted to do. But that was the key. She knew what she wanted.

Nathan was waiting for me to answer. I had cross-country, but missing one practice wouldn't hurt, I thought, deciding I was too tired anyway for the work-out to do me any good. A jolt of caffeine was what I needed, to give me the energy to tackle my homework. You can justify anything.

"Okay," I said, hoping I sounded casual, and walked back to the group with Nathan.

Everything that followed was like an out-of-body experience, from walking down the main drag of Galloway to the time in the restaurant. They did it all so easily, so smoothly, this bantering and laughing. They all made a real effort to include me, too. Nathan even paid for my Coke.

"Enjoy it while it lasts," Nicole laughed. "Nathan's pretty tight-fisted."

"A fool and his money are soon parted, and I'm no fool," Nathan said.

From this, I understood two things. One, I might be asked back; and two, if I was, I'd be expected to pay my own way. That was fine with me. Everyone else in the group paid for themselves. I'd be on equal terms.

No one mentioned Casey. They asked me about my weekend job and I told them about changing smelly sheets in the nursing home. Someone made a joke about old people and that set off a whole series of dumb jokes, really stupid. But I laughed anyway.

The group made fun of the other customers and spilled sugar on the table deliberately, to "make the waitress work for her paycheck." They re-hashed the school day, caught me up with who was dating who, and passed on gossip about the teachers. Really, they talked about nothing at all. And I enjoyed it. I couldn't truly relax, because I was on probation with them, but I was laughing in all the right places and even holding my own in the conversation.

I said something insulting about the old man at the table across the room and everyone laughed, as though I'd said something really clever.

No one asked me what I was reading. No one brought up anything they'd seen on the news and asked me what I thought about it. No one asked me how my cross-country training was going. No one asked me what I cared about. It was all very, very easy.

In the middle of this, a thought came into my head, clear and bold as a newspaper headline: *You're the one who's been keeping me from the group all these years*, I thought. *Damn you, Casey.*

We parted all friendly at the end of an hour. Nathan walked partway home with me before veering down Spruce Street to his own home.

"See you tomorrow," he yelled after me. I wasn't

sure about that—good things never last—but I felt much lighter than I had in weeks, and my feet bounced a little as I walked the rest of the way home.

My feet stopped bouncing when I got to my house. Another letter from Casey was waiting for me on the hall table.

THIRTEEN

Dear Dragonfly,

How are you holding up out there? For some reason, your letters aren't getting through. Mela is trying to find out what the problem is. I'd find all this so much easier if they'd let me hear from you.

I'll bet Galloway is an interesting place right now. Mela tells me the town is like a circus, with me in the center ring. Since you're my best friend, you must be getting a lot of nasty attention. Try to remember that Galloway is still just Galloway, even if it looks like a circus right now.

The guards have been letting me outside lately, but only for one hour a day, and then only to a concrete yard. But there are bugs everywhere, even on concrete!

Two days ago a black swallowtail, *Papilio polyxenes*, flew over the wall and landed on my shoulder. It sat there looking lovely until a guard scared it away. Yesterday I found a cricket, *Gryllus veletis*, and brought him to my cell. He sang to me all night. I put him in a bit of water in my sink and watched the horsehair worms crawl out of him. Gross...fantastic! Fabulous! I set him free during today's outdoor period. One of us locked up is more than enough.

I've developed a bit of a friendship with a colony of pavement ants, *Tretramrium caespitum*, that's made its home in the cracks of the pavement. I think we have a connection. The colony is mostly made up of female ants that will never have babies. I used to think it would be fun to have a kid-remember how we would talk about it? I'd strap her to my back and head out into the field, and as she got older she would help me collect specimens. I'd teach her all about bugs. I don't think I could do that now. What if something happened to her? How do people carry their grief when they lose a child? How does Mrs. Glass get out of bed every day—first she loses her husband to a drunk driver, and now Stephanie.

Stephanie was a little monster, but she probably would have grown out of that. I wish I'd tried harder to like her. Maybe she wouldn't be dead now if I had.

They're still keeping me away from the other prisoners, but I talk to the ones who bring me meals and they seem like nice people. Mela comes a lot, and that helps. She usually does environmental law, so we have a lot to talk about, when she has time. I'm sure more than ever now that I want to specialize in aquatic insects. They give us clues to the health of a pond's ecosystem, and, as we all know, ground water is everything! Mela says that when I get out of here, she'll arrange for me to meet some folks from the environmental science department at her old university. She says they lead field trips all the time and I might be able to go on one. It will make up a bit for missing Australia.

They've set a trial date for late in January. I'm going to be in here for a while. Mom and Dad try to be cheerful when they come to see me, so I try to be cheerful, too. But it gets harder and harder each time. This is a nightmare.

Your mom has been so great to my folks! Please thank her for me, although I know she doesn't want any thanks. She's done so much for me over the years. She helped me track down books I needed, she put me in touch with people at the university scholarship department, she helped me get a microscope—well, you know.

How is your running going this fall? Don't worry so much about me that your grades start falling or you let cross-country slip. I'll get out of this mess, make up the lost time at school, and still go to university with you next fall. I'm counting on you not to let down your end of our plans!

I'm running out of room again. Hey, did you notice that I'm allowed two sheets of paper instead of just one? If the taxpayers only knew!

Keep your wings up, Dragonfly. Write soon!

With love,
Casey

I knew I wasn't going to answer this letter either.

I went up to my room and flopped down on my bed, still unmade from that morning when I'd been in such a fog. Casey thought I was worrying so much about her that I wasn't paying attention to my schoolwork, that I wasn't doing my best in cross-country! She just assumed I'd put my life on hold in order to worry about her. The arrogance of that! I had plenty of other things in my life besides my friendship with Casey! Plenty!

Into my resentment, another thought came. All those things she wrote about my mother doing things for her—I hadn't known about a single one of them. Mom didn't know how to track down books. She didn't know anyone at the university. What did she know about microscopes? Mom didn't know about operating in the important world. She was just a nursing home housekeeper—lots of times she was even too crazy to do that. Casey had to be joking.

But Casey never made jokes about my mother. She knew a side to Mom that I had never guessed at. It reminded me that I had another reason to be mad at her.

I hated her.

And yet I ached for her.

That night I was determined to sleep through. When I woke up at two a.m., I stayed in bed. My legs wanted to be cycling but I wouldn't let them. I did everything I could think of to get back to sleep, but it was at least four o'clock before I drifted off. Then I kept dreaming that I was falling, waking up just before I hit the ground, then dozing off to sleep again. For all the rest I got, I might as well have gone biking.

The next day after school, I went out to the restaurant with the group again. We still didn't talk about Casey. We didn't really talk about anything, but I enjoyed myself. I barely felt guilty about ducking out of cross-country. There would be time later to think up an excuse for the coach.

Mom was quiet at dinner. She just picked at her food. I could have asked her what was wrong but I didn't really want to know. I don't think Dad noticed.

I went biking that night. *Why fight it*, I thought, when two a.m. rolled around again. At least I'd get some of the exercise I missed by skipping practice.

After cycling aimlessly around town for a while, I biked up Casey's street. As I got closer to the house, I noticed something was going on. I dropped my bike noiselessly behind a neighbor's forsythia and crept over for a closer look.

Some kids were vandalizing Casey's house. They had poured paint all over her father's wheelchair van and were throwing paint at the windows and walls of the house. I could smell the oil in the paint. The kids had brought gallons and gallons of it.

Two of the kids were painting something on the road in front of the house. "Hurry up!" somebody whispered. Someone else muffled a laugh.

They left the paint cans littering the yard and street, got in their car, and drove past me. The light from the street lamp caught their faces as they drove by. It was the group from The Cactus. Amber spotted me in the bushes. She did the double finger-gun gesture at me as they sped off into the night.

I walked over and took a look at the destruction they'd left. Toxic paint was soaking into the lawn, flower-erbeds, and into the bricks of the house. The van was covered in florescent yellow. On the street, in big letters, with an arrow pointing at the house, they had written, "KILLER CASEY LIVED HERE."

I was too stunned to move. The sheer magnitude of the mess was overwhelming. It held me spellbound until I heard a noise. It was probably just a cat looking for some garbage, but it startled me. I ran back to my bike and got out of there.

It wasn't until the next morning that I realized there was paint on one of my sneakers. I must have stepped in some by accident. I only had one pair of sneakers. I couldn't afford to throw them out. Frantically, I checked the rest of the house for paint footprints. But I didn't find any.

I heard the front door slam. Mom had just come back in. I knew without asking where she'd been.

"I hate this town!" she wailed. "I hate this town! I hate these people!"

I joined her in the kitchen to see if I could calm her down. "It's all right, Mom."

She spun on me. "It is not all right. How dare you say it is? First, their own church shuns the Whites. That wheelchair ramp hasn't been put back up. I keep trying to get hold of Reverend Fleet but he won't come to the phone when I call. His secretary and his wife say he's out whenever I drop by his office or the manse. Out, my foot. He's there, hiding under the pulpit! Christianity stands for courage—I pity him when he gets to the pearly gates."

"Then the Whites start getting threatening letters. Michael White, a hero in this town, and Linda White, who's been a support to everyone who ever needed one…and now this!"

"What do you mean?" I asked.

In answer, she took me by the arm and force-marched me all the way over to the Whites' house.

By the light of day it looked even worse.

The Cactus gang had chosen the brightest, most garish colors in the spectrum. Lime green all over the red bricks of the house. Bright orange over the windows and the wheelchair ramp. Pink all over the lawns and gardens. And that hideous yellow on the van and the street.

A police car was parked at the curb across the street from the Whites' house. I spotted the officer a short ways down the block, talking to a woman on her front porch who was shaking her head and probably saying, "No, I didn't see anything." A few other neighbors were out on their lawns, staring and frowning. No one was offering to help clean it up.

A large puddle of paint was congealing on the pavement. Struck with an idea of sudden brilliance, I walked over to it, pretending to want a closer look at the damage, and stuck my shoe in the wet paint.

"Watch where you're walking!" Mom shrieked. I pulled my foot away quickly. Now I had an explanation for the paint on my shoes. Now I was safe.

I'd known without even thinking about it that I wouldn't report Amber and the others. They could have easily said I was part of it, and then it would be the six of them against me. That wasn't the main reason I'd keep my mouth shut, though. The main reason was this: if I squealed, they wouldn't invite me back to The Cactus with them.

And then I'd be alone again.

FOUR-TEEN

Mom really began to get ill after that. The vandalizing of the Whites' home broke through any illusions she was able to hold onto that Galloway would somehow come to its senses and become a decent place to live again. She was angry at everybody.

Well, no, that's not exactly accurate. I was with her sometimes in the nursing home. She'd come in to help me strip beds or carry stinking sheets to the laundry room, and she'd be just as kind and gentle as a saint. She'd go over to some old lady who was crying with embarrassment and have her feeling good again in two seconds flat. She wasn't patronizing, either, the way some of the other nurses were, talking to the old people as if they were small children. She knew all the residents' names, too, and knew things about them the nurses didn't.

Back out in the street, though, she let everybody have it. She didn't discriminate. We were in the grocery store the Saturday after the incident. Mom went up and down the aisles, starting arguments with every shopper she met.

"Do you think Casey White is guilty?" she asked.

The shoppers, surprised by the question in the middle of reaching for their Captain Crunch or their pork luncheon meat, would answer truthfully, "Yes, I think she did it." Then Mom would let them have it—old or young, small children in the cart or not, she didn't care.

I had to take her arms several times and pull her away from people. One man in particular looked like he was about to hit her. I pulled her away more for his safety than hers. When Mom gets going, she's more than a match for anybody.

I could tell in an instant who knew Mom and who didn't. Those who didn't know about her actually started engaging her in discussion. Those who knew her—well, I saw their eyes glaze over and their faces grow tolerant as soon as they realized that Mom was off on one of her tirades.

It's just Vivian gone mad again was what their expressions said, and they excused themselves as quickly as possible. This, strangely, made her even angrier than those who argued with her. By the time we got to the checkout, she was beyond all boundaries of rationality. The poor girl working the cash register, a girl who was a grade behind me in school, got the full force of it. Nothing I could do would calm Mom down. Everyone was staring at us.

Finally, the manager called the police and Mom was escorted onto the sidewalk. The cashier was too upset to continue ringing up our groceries, so the manager sent her back to the locker room to compose herself while he finished up. All the while, Mom was pressed up against the plate-glass window, banging it and yelling at everyone.

"Don't bring her in here again," the manager said to me as he handed me my change. "You got that?"

I wanted to argue that I could no more control my mother's behavior than he could, but I just nodded, picked up the groceries, and walked out.

"Let's go home, Mom," I said, trying to nudge her away from the window.

She spun around and snapped at me. "How can you condone them? Who *are* you?"

I left her and went home by myself. We had walked to the grocery store and the bags I carried were heavy. By the time I got home there were deep red welts in my fingers where the bag handles had pressed into my skin.

Dad and I walked on eggshells after that.

"Can't you do something?" I asked him that evening. Mom had not prepared anything for supper, so Dad and I had driven to Hamburger World on the edge of town. We took our food over to a picnic table.

"It's not time yet," he replied. "She'll never agree to go voluntarily, and they won't commit her unless they can prove she's a danger to herself or others. You know that." He bit into his burger, I think, to avoid having to say anything more.

"You should have seen her in the grocery store," I said. "I've never seen her like that, not even in the early days. There was something different about her, more focused than usual, maybe. I don't know."

I kept describing the incident, even though I knew Dad didn't want to hear it. He even turned himself away to try to deflect my words before they reached his ears. I told him things I usually only told Casey.

I always told Casey about Mom's strange behavior. Often, she was there to witness it, and we would discuss it after. When I said all I needed to say, Casey would say, "You think that's strange, well, let me tell you about the shore fly, which actually breeds in puddles of crude oil." Off she'd go, describing one of her insect friends. Sometimes that was annoying, but I could always count on it, and that made it comforting. Mom was strange, but she was only one of the many strange things in this universe. No big deal.

I talked on and on to Dad about Mom, but Dad had nothing comforting to say. He had no newspaper to hide behind so he took a tremendous interest in the cars going by on the highway.

Dad started giving me supper money every morning before he left for work. He stayed late at his job, which saved him from dealing with either Mom or me. I was grateful for the money. I used it at The Cactus after school. The kids kept asking me and I kept accepting. They didn't mention Casey and I didn't mention Paint Night. It was expensive, belonging to the good crowd, and I hated having to use the money I worked so hard for, so the regular handouts from Dad really helped.

Things started disappearing from the house. Mom had been taking casseroles and muffins over to the Whites for a while, but that was no longer enough for her. She emptied all the food from our cupboards and took it to Casey's house. She took them other things as well—our good china, the toaster oven, lamps, my old toys, anything she could carry. It's like she was saying, "Here, take this, let me try to make up for all the bad things the town is doing to you." Dad made frequent trips to the Whites' to pick up our stuff.

The days went by like that. I'm tempted to say they fell into a routine, just for the convenience of saying that, but there was nothing routine about those days. The only thing I could count on was waking up at two o'clock each morning.

FIFTEEN

A few days later, I had two encounters with teachers, neither of them pleasant.

The first was with Ms. Simms, the cross-country coach. I'd successfully avoided her for over a week, since I'd started going to the restaurant after school instead of to practice, but that morning she came right into my history class. She must have worked out an arrangement with the history teacher beforehand, because as soon as she showed up at the door, he sent me out into the hallway to talk to her.

"What's going on?" Ms. Simms asked, in her usual direct way.

Beating about the bush with her would have been a waste of time. For such a small town, Galloway sure had a lot of strong-willed women.

"I'm busy after school," I replied.

"You're hanging out with losers," she said. "They're just high-school popular. It's all smoke, no substance. It doesn't translate into anything in real life."

"They're my friends," I protested feebly.

"Friends would insist you show up for practice," Ms. Simms said. "These kids use people. They want something from you, but you won't believe me, so let's not waste time with that. Here is my message. Start showing up for practice or I'll drop you from the team."

She didn't have to elaborate. No team meant no chance at a scholarship. No scholarship meant no university. I didn't want to be a gym teacher but I did want to get out of town. A scholarship was my easy escape.

"I'll train in the mornings," I promised.

Ms. Simms didn't like my answer but she decided to accept it. "I'm at school by seven-thirty anyway," she said. "I expect to see you waiting for me in the parking lot when I arrive. Be dressed and ready to work out. If you miss a day, or you're late, you'll be cut from the team." She spun on her heel and headed back to the gym.

I didn't blame Ms. Simms for being angry with me. She'd put in a lot of time with me over the years, helping me train. She'd gone out of her way many times, especially when Mom was ill, to make sure I got a ride to track meets and that I had the proper clothes and shoes.

The thought of training in the morning didn't thrill me. Since I'd stopped sleeping through the night, I was sleeping until the last possible minute in the mornings. I'd have to get up at six-thirty to get to school on time. Ms. Simms didn't fool around. She wouldn't give me another chance if I blew this one.

The second teacher encounter came just as I was about to have lunch. I had fifteen minutes to eat after my cafeteria shift ended and my next class began. I had just sat down with my tray when the announcement came over the public address system: "Would Jessica Harris please report to Miss Burke in Room 313."

I groaned, not in the mood for another lecture about my poor academic performance, but a summons was a summons. I quickly shoveled spaghetti into my mouth, washed it down with some milk, and ate my apple on the way to the biology lab, even though eating in the hallway was against the rules. I dropped the apple core into a trashcan just outside the classroom.

Miss Burke looked up as I entered. Her face was pale. "Jessica, thank you for coming so quickly."

"Are you all right?" One doesn't usually ask such questions of teachers. If they're ill, it's none of our business, but she looked so ghostly and troubled it just popped out of me.

"No, Jessica, I'm not all right, but I'm hoping you

can help me. Close the door, please."

My last biology quiz had come back with an okay grade, so I didn't understand what she was getting at.

"Come back into the storage room. I have something for you."

I followed her into the small room off the biology classroom, where extra supplies and things were stored. Casey was the only student trusted with a key to this room. I had helped her clean and organize it one Saturday.

The first things I noticed were the glass cases displaying the large insect collection Casey had caught and pinned for the school. I hadn't even noticed that the cases had been taken down from the classroom walls.

Miss Burke saw me looking at them. "I thought they'd be safer locked in here, given the current mood of the school," she said, running her hands gently over the glass. Casey's father had made the cases in his woodworking shop. There were more of them in Casey's house.

"I've been teaching for forty-three years," Miss Burke said. "I've never met a student with a scientific curiosity to equal Casey's. She's the type of student a teacher will spend her whole career hoping to come across. Casey takes such joy from learning things! You're her friend, so you know this, but I wonder if you truly appreciate how gifted she is. She could be a pioneer, a

Jane Goodall of the insect world. But now there's this dreadful mess."

I didn't know what to say, so I said nothing. To my horror, Miss Burke began to cry.

"You should hear the things they say about her in the staff room. Teachers are supposed to be enlightened people, but they sound like they come from the Dark Ages. And I haven't done anything to help Casey. I spoke up for her once, but my colleagues said I was only trying to secure my legacy, that if Casey was guilty it meant that all the years I've put in have been for nothing—no star pupil, no lasting impact. I am ashamed that I allowed their comments to silence me. Why should I care what they think? I know in my heart what is true."

I didn't know what to do. Should I pat her shoulder to comfort her? That didn't seem appropriate, so I just stood there with my hands in my pockets, feeling inadequate, embarrassed and angry at having been put in this position.

Miss Burke composed herself without my help, drying her tears with a snowy-white linen handkerchief.

"But I don't have to continue to be ashamed," she said. "I'm not going to sit back and let them take Casey's academic year from her. And this is where you come in. I'd like you to find out from Casey's parents if she can continue with her studies while she's in jail. If she can, I'll arrange with her other teachers to get course assignments to her. She's bound to be found not guilty at her trial, and if she can keep up with her studies, she can still graduate this year and get a science scholarship, like we'd planned. Her trip to Australia—well, there will be other opportunities, other trips. It's a shame, though. She worked so hard for it."

She turned away and pulled something out of a drawer. "Also, see if they can get this book to Casey. I know how fond she is of beetles."

Miss Burke handed me a very large book called, *The World of Beetles*. It was just the sort of book Casey would drool over, with close-up photos of hundreds of beetles doing all the strange things they do.

The bell rang. I could hear kids coming into the classroom after the lunch break.

"Thank you, Jessica," Miss Burke said. "You're a good friend. Maybe now I can start looking at myself in the mirror again."

Class began. I hid the beetle book inside my binder so that no one would ask me about it. Anyone who saw me with an insect book would know it was for Casey, and I didn't need that.

The gang at the restaurant found it, though. Nicole grabbed my binder to check on the work assigned for History and, of course, pulled the bug book out for everyone to see.

"What's this?" she asked, as if she deserved an explanation. "You taking up the Weird One's hobby?"

Up until that moment, The Cactus gang had completely refrained from mentioning Casey in my presence. When I was with them, I was almost able to forget Casey existed. Now, suddenly, she was at the table with us. I began to panic.

"Old Lady Burke gave it to me to take to Casey's parents," I said.

"You're not going to do it, are you?"

I had to come up with something fast. "Well, my bio grades have been slipping. She kind of hinted that she'd give me a break if I did her this favor." Then I told the group about our discussion in the storage room, playing up the crying scene to make them laugh.

"She's senile," Nicole said. "They would have fired her years ago if she hadn't had union protection."

"It's not surprising that she likes Casey so much," Amber said, stirring sugar into her Diet Coke. She did that every day, and the clink of the spoon against her glass annoyed me. "They're two of a kind."

I took the bait. I shouldn't have, but I did. "Both crazy about bugs?"

"Well, sure, but more important, they're both *not* crazy about boys."

"You mean Miss Burke is a dyke?" Nathan asked with a grin.

"Duh!" Amber frowned. "*Miss* Burke! Never married, all those stories in class about traveling the world with other old-maid science teachers. You don't think they just crawled around looking at bugs, do you?"

"Oh, that is so gross!" Nicole sputtered. "Burke is so old and ugly!"

"She wasn't always old," Cliff, another group member, pointed out. "I say, God bless and go to it."

"You *would*!" Amber said. "But I think it's scandalous, allowing her to teach all these years, having contact with female students. We should report her to someone." Amber turned to me. "Is that what made Casey gay, Jess—or was she gay before?"

"I…I don't know," I stammered. "I guess I really don't know her that well."

"You'd better not be gay," Nicole said.

"Yeah—we'd have to kill you." Nathan said this and laughed, but I wasn't sure he was joking. "Gay people should all be killed. Hitler was right about that."

That started the gang off, listing all the other people Hitler should have killed when he had the chance—game-show contestants, slow waitresses, chess-club members—and I breathed a sigh of relief that the attention was off me.

Shortly after, I excused myself and went into the ladies' room. I kept my head down while I was washing my hands. I washed them over, and over, and over.

SIXTEEN

Are you getting enough of a story? Or are you getting tired of it? I see you looking at your watch—and you're jiggling your coffee cup. You can go if you want to. I know I said there's a lot you don't know, but maybe you don't have to hear it after all. The door's not locked. No one is holding you against your will.

So go, if you're going to, but stop wasting my time pretending you've got to be somewhere at this hour. It's four in the morning, the hour of nothing and we're in the middle of nowhere. But march out into it, if you want to. Leave before I finish my next sentence. I don't care about manners.

But you won't, will you? You won't go because my story isn't finished and because I'm a minor celebrity, and it makes you feel special to be hearing my story.

* * *

I dropped by Casey's home later that afternoon, knowing that if I delayed it by even an hour, I'd never do it.

Mrs. White came to the door. There was some reservation in her greeting, and she did not ask me in.

"Michael is not well. He misses Casey, and it's difficult to get him to the jail since those vandals poured paint in the gas tank of the van." She sighed heavily and ran a hand through her hair, pushing it off her face. "Every day I call the police to see if they've caught the people who did this to us, and every day they tell me to be patient."

She brightened a little when I gave her the beetle book and said she'd tell Casey's lawyer to arrange things at the detention center to allow her schoolwork in.

She had a few kind words for Miss Burke, and then she said, "I know people are backing you into a corner, Jess, getting you to say things you don't mean. I hope things get easier for you soon."

I wanted to hug her but she stayed half-hidden behind the door. I could smell chicken stew cooking on the stove. Mrs. White did not ask me to stay for dinner. I went home.

I reported to Miss Burke before classes started the next morning. She was delighted to learn she could get schoolwork to Casey through Mela Cross. Her face suddenly looked younger, and I remember thinking what a powerful thing forgiveness is. Miss Burke was forgiving herself for not speaking out about Casey sooner. Her spine, curved in the way that happens sometimes with old ladies, actually straightened out a bit.

"I'll talk to her other teachers today," she said. "Thank you, Jessica. You are a real friend to Casey, and that's something to be proud of. I'm sure it hasn't been easy for you. It will probably get harder once the trial starts, but you won't mind that, will you? That's the price of friendship. I have had a few close friends in my life, too, women who have known me better than I knew myself—"

The five-minute bell rang and I had to excuse myself and hurry to class. Before I left, she grabbed my shoulder with her old-woman hand and gave it a squeeze. I could feel her hand on me all the rest of the day. She did it to express her support, but all it did was remind me what a coward I was.

At lunchtime, I was working on the checkout line in the cafeteria when Nathan pushed himself forward.

"To the back of the line, young man," the lunch supervisor ordered.

Nathan stepped aside to let me keep checking people through while he talked.

"I just came from the teachers' lounge," he said.

"They let you in the teachers' lounge?"

"No, no, outside of it. There was a ferocious argument going on inside, about your friend Casey."

I didn't like the way he said, "your friend Casey." It made me feel involved in a way I didn't want to be. Still, Nathan was someone who for years had never even acknowledged that I was human. And he must be answered if I was to avoid going back to sub-human status.

"What about Casey?"

"You won't believe this. Old Lady Burke was defending her, practically screaming at the other teachers. She was yelling so loud, a lot of students could hear."

"Miss Burke?" I couldn't believe it. Miss Burke never raised her voice.

"Burke was yelling that the other teachers should hand over their course work to Casey while she was locked up, that anyone who didn't should be ashamed of themselves. She said that Casey is the most talented student to ever attend Galloway High. Some of the other teachers yelled back that they wouldn't lift a finger to help a child killer. And then it got personal."

I was so absorbed in what Nathan was saying, I let several kids through the line without charging them for their tuna surprise, then I took someone's money and had to be prodded into giving them change.

"One of the teachers, I think it was Higgins, yelled

that Burke was clearly senile and needed to be in a home, and another woman—I couldn't tell who—yelled that she was going to go to the principal because someone as warped as Burke shouldn't be around children."

"And then what happened?"

"And then the vice-principal appeared and chewed me out for loitering in the hall, so I rushed down here to tell you."

I was flattered that he'd told me before he told anyone else, until he told me the reason.

"I figured you might know something."

I shrugged. "I guess Casey's other teachers don't like her as much as Old Burke does."

"She sure flipped out."

"I've got her class right after lunch," I said. "If she says or does anything else strange, I'll let you know."

Nathan said he'd meet me later and I got on with my job. I felt important. I was a sort of spy for the group.

Miss Burke wasn't in the biology room when I got to class. Ten minutes into the period, she still wasn't there. The classroom buzzed with speculation. News of the fight in the teachers' lounge had gotten around. Kids were saying things like, "Maybe she's been fired." "Maybe she had a heart attack." None of us came close to imagining what was really going on, but we soon found out.

Miss Burke's voice came over the loudspeaker. "Good afternoon, students," she began. "I'm sorry to interrupt your classes, but I need to speak to all of you about one of your schoolmates. I need to speak to you about Casey White.

"There's been a lot of foolish talk branding Casey as a murderer. Lots of people in this town—and, I'm ashamed to say, inside this school—are jumping on the Casey-is-guilty bandwagon. I want you to stop and think now. Put down your books and your pens, listen to me, and think.

"Have any of you ever been wrongly accused? Do you remember what a frustrating, lonely place that is? People who you thought were your friends accusing you? People turning on you, eager to believe the worst? Didn't you want to say to them, 'But it's me! You know me! You know I wouldn't do such a thing!' Maybe you even did say that, but it didn't do any good.

"You all know Casey White. Many of you have gone to school with her since the third grade. You know she is not the sort of person who could commit this horrible crime. Casey is part of our school community. She has won awards for this school with her scientific pursuits. She has distinguished herself and brought honor to this school. And now she is being treated with dishonor."

The classroom door slammed open. We all jumped.

"Miss Burke has locked herself in the intercom office!" a kid yelled out and then ran down the hall spreading the news.

I was the first one out the door, but others were close behind me. By the time we reached the office door, a crowd of students had already gathered. Teachers tried to chase them back to their classrooms, but everyone ignored them.

Miss Burke kept talking about Casey's accomplishments, her good spirit, her generous nature. Everything she said was met with derision by the crowd. Someone even shouted out that ridiculous nursery rhyme, "Miss Burke and Casey, sitting in a tree, K.I.S.S.I.N.G..."

Students kept spilling into the hallway. I could hear the principal's booming voice on the edge of the crowd, trying to push through to the office, probably with an extra set of keys, but no one would let him pass.

"Detentions will be given out!" teachers warned.

No one cared.

Miss Burke kept talking. "I have been on this Earth for many more years than any of you, more than anyone else in this school. I have seen injustices visited upon the world by greed and ignorance. I have seen the world explode in war and witnessed the sad march of humanity struggle with starvation and unnatural disaster. Throughout the whole sad history of the human race, there have been moments when things could have gone the other way, when individuals could have chosen a different path and raised us up out of the mud."

And then something started happening to the kids crowded in the hallway. They began to quiet down. Miss Burke was starting to turn them. Soon, the only voices that could be heard—other than Miss Burke's—were the teachers yelling at us to get back to class.

"A school is a community, just like a town or a city. The world outside has an impact on us, like it does on any town or city, but we have an advantage. We are an enclosed community. We can set our own standards. We have a chance to be better in here than the world is outside. Do we dare to take that chance? Are we brave enough?

"I think we are. I think the students of Galloway High can rise above the garbage that the world throws at us—the lies and the simplistic solutions. We can become better than the world, and we can start to do that right now.

"We can begin by putting a higher value on friendship than the world wants us to. Casey White is our friend. She has not been found guilty of any crime and I don't believe she ever will be. We can refuse to abandon her. We can stand with her, the way we would want our friends to stand with us if we were ever in trouble."

"Cops!" someone cried, and, sure enough, the police were suddenly in the hallway, shoving and even lifting students out of the way. They cleared a path for the principal. Kids booed and threw stuff at him as he approached the office door with his keys. Books and school supplies—even shoes—flew through the air. The police didn't bother to seek out the culprits. They pushed and hit anyone they could reach. I don't know if the kids were upset because the principal was about to silence Miss Burke, or because he was breaking up the fun. I still don't know.

Several cops went into the office with the principal. They even had their guns drawn. The intercom office was a small room inside the larger office. How Miss Burke had managed to clear and lock both offices, I'll never know.

We could hear her being pulled from her seat in front of the microphone. We heard one of the cops begin to place her under arrest, and then the intercom cut off. It took only a moment for them to bring her out.

The principal led the way, frowning. The cops were huge men in dark navy with their caps pulled low over their foreheads. Miss Burke was handcuffed behind her back, the way Casey had been. Two cops, one on each side, held her arms tightly. At first glance, she looked small and pale between them.

The crowd of kids hooted and applauded as she was

taken away. Again, I don't know if it was in appreciation for her speech or for the show. She didn't acknowledge any of us. She walked calmly and proudly between the two cops, who had the good grace to look slightly embarrassed at having to keep a strong grip on a tiny, old, handcuffed lady in a lace-trimmed flower-print dress.

I looked more closely. Miss Burke was not small at all. She was tall, tall. Her head was high and her eyes were sparkling. She was smiling, and in that moment, she looked thirty years younger.

We got a substitute the next day. We were informed that Miss Burke would not be returning. The substitute found Casey's insect collection in the storage room and put it up on display in the classroom. Next afternoon, all the cases had been smashed on the floor, the insects ground up on the linoleum. The substitute ranted and railed, but no one helped him clean up the mess. Not even me.

August 29

Day 9

Casey and I plan some activities for the sleep-out, but it is almost the end of camp and everyone is sick of being organized. The kids are tired and by the time we get the sleep-out space set up and wood gathered for the fire, they are content to sit around and talk and eat. Hot dogs sizzle in the coals, marshmallows catch on fire, and the combined smells of wood smoke and summer night are delicious.

By the beam of a flashlight Casey finishes the bedtime book we've been reading aloud to the kids since camp started. We are reading *From Anna* by Jean Little. At the very end, Anna sings "Silent Night," and the campers usually start singing, too. That's what happens this time, and we work our way through Christmas carols and the usual list of camp songs until the singing gradually winds down. Talking takes its place, the sort of truth telling that happens best when you get around a campfire. The kids talk about bullies at school, problems with their parents, grandparents they've lost—the usual things.

Stephanie behaves through all of this, until the girl next to her asks her to stop hogging all the space on the ground sheet. She starts kicking and throwing sticks and pinecones in the fire so that sparks fly around. We tell her to knock it off. She sulks and moves her sleeping bag to a space a few yards outside the circle. We can see her still, off pouting in the shadows, so we ignore her, glad that she's quiet. That's where she is when Mrs. Keefer appears with a thermos of hot chocolate, and that's where she is when I almost trip over her in the middle of the night on my way to the latrine.

One of the campers, Deanna Brown, wakes me up after that because she has a stomachache. She is clutching her right side, doubled over in pain, and she is burning with fever. I know first aid well enough not to mess around. I quickly whisper to Casey that I am taking Deanna to the camp nurse. I scoop Deanna up in my arms and run as fast as I can down the trail that leads to the Bone House. The sky is black-dark and the air has a predawn heaviness to it. I don't notice if

Stephanie is still in her spot or not. I don't think about Stephanie at all.

I kick at the door of the infirmary. Bones answers in her nightgown. Behind her, I can see that sick kids occupy several of the beds. She takes one look at Deanna and presses her car keys into my hand.

"Get her to Emergency," she says. "Don't waste a second. I'll call ahead and tell them you're coming. I'll call her parents, too. Go!"

Bones keeps her car right outside the infirmary. She helps me load Deanna in.

"There are quarters in the ashtray," she says. "Keep me posted."

I take off. I break all speed limits but there are no other cars on the road. The clock on the dashboard reads 2:00 a.m. I get Deanna to the hospital in Galloway in record time. They take out her appendix just before it bursts.

I call Bones and she says the parents are on their way in. They live a few hours away and could I wait at the hospital until they get there? Deanna might need to see a familiar face.

I sit in the waiting room, dozing over an old copy of *Good Housekeeping*, and finally stretch out on one of the plastic orange sofas.

"Are you Jessica?"

The voice brings me out of my sleep. Standing in front of me is a middle-aged couple wearing rumpled and mismatched clothes obviously thrown on in a hurry.

I stand up quickly, get a head rush, and have to sit back down again. "I'm Jess," I manage to say.

"We're Deanna's parents," the man says. "The doctor tells us if you had waited a moment longer to get her to the hospital, she might not have made it. We want to thank you."

I stand back up. "How's she doing?"

"She's sleeping. She's out of danger," the man says.

"She'll want to thank you herself when she wakes up," the woman says. "You're our family's hero now. If only more teenagers were like you."

They return to their daughter and I sit back on the plastic sofa. I rub my eyes and think about being a hero. I decide to wait around until Deanna wakes up. Today is the last day of camp, the campers will be heading home soon, and I don't care about any one of them enough to want to say goodbye.

Maybe Deanna's parents will offer me some cash as a reward for my quick-thinking actions. I'll turn it down, of course, but they will insist, and to make them feel better I'll accept. Maybe they will tell the newspapers, too. *Camp Counselor Saves Child's Life.* Let my mother try to find something to criticize about that! Maybe the summer will end on a high note after all.

I sit with this thought for a while and stare out the window at the rain, which is falling in sheets. It must have started while I was asleep. I picture Casey scrambling to get the campers out of the rain and to get their gear packed and carried back down the trail. All the kids will head home today with their sleeping bags soaked and their shoes full of mud. For once, I am the hero and Casey is doing the dirty work.

The rain will get in the way of our end-of-camp plans, but maybe we can get permission to stay in one of the cabins, or maybe in the infirmary, which has loads of dry sheets and blankets. If that's a no, then I'll go to Casey's house for a couple of days. We'll still get a chance to unwind before school starts.

Finally, I decide I'd better call in to Bones.

"We have a situation," she says. "You need to get back here right away. Stephanie is missing."

"Of course she is," I say.

"No, she's really missing."

"She's just hiding," I say. "She knows camp is over this morning. She's taking one last opportunity to bug us."

"She was gone when the rest of Cabin Three woke up this morning. We've been searching for two hours. There's no sign of her and the rain just keeps coming down."

I am going to suggest that Stephanie is probably up in the mess-hall pantry, warm and dry and eating fistfuls of cereal out of a box—we've caught her doing that before—but Bones doesn't give me a chance. She just says, "We need you back here," and hangs up.

I slam the receiver back against the pay phone. I am in no hurry to head back to camp. Once I arrive they'll put me right to work, if not looking for Stephanie then helping my cabin kids pack up and get ready for their parents.

The clock says 8:45. By the time I get back, breakfast will be cleaned up and done. I decide to have breakfast at the hospital.

I wander around the wards until I see a cart full of food trays. The nurses are busy. I peek inside a couple of the trays, find one that doesn't look too putrid, and walk away with it, tossing the name-tag into a garbage bin. I sit back on my orange plastic couch. The eggs are almost the same color.

"That can't be good," I mutter, but I eat them anyway, and I slather the toast with jam from the little packets. I take my time drinking the apple juice. I even wash up in the ladies' room off the waiting room. I am sure that Stephanie will have appeared by the time I get back to camp.

This is not something I can take seriously.

The rain is coming down quite heavily and the temperature has plummeted. Summer's over, I think, as I rush from the hospital to the car. Back at camp I get my rain jacket out of the cabin before going, as directed, to the sleep-out clearing.

Casey is standing with a group of very worried-looking people. Mrs. Keefer is talking on her cell phone. Casey is drenched, even in her rain gear, and is looking as annoyed as I feel.

"So, you finally killed her off, eh?" I ask, laughing.

Casey grins. "And I stuffed her body in a hollow tree."

The cold silence that greets these remarks makes me wish I'd kept my mouth shut, especially when I notice that one of the frowning people is a police officer. An explanation would only have made things worse, so I clear my throat and try to get into the spirit of the search.

We search all morning, getting wetter and more miserable as the rain and temperatures continue to fall. We are in an autumn rainstorm, not a summer shower. More police arrive to join in the effort. There is talk of bringing in search dogs, but that's not possible while it is raining so hard.

By midday, Casey and I are furious. We take a short lunch break together in the field, hot chocolate from a thermos and sandwiches brought out by the kitchen staff. We eat the sandwiches quickly but they still get soaked with rainwater.

"I hate that kid," I say. "She's ruined the last day of camp for everyone."

"If she's not dead when we find her, I'm going

to kill her myself," Casey says, then suddenly stops, her mouth open in mid-chew. She is staring over my left shoulder.

I turn around. Behind me is Stephanie's mother. From the look on her face, I know she has heard every word we have said.

SEVEN-TEEN

Casey became a regular topic of conversation at The Cactus. Miss Burke's actions meant that the subject was fair game. It should have struck me as strange that they had only mentioned Casey once before, but it didn't. I truly thought they were interested in me as a person, not just a ticket to the media circus surrounding Casey.

Okay, maybe I didn't *really* think they were all that innocent, but I chose to ignore what I really thought. I chose to lie to myself and pretend we were all friends together.

The gang started asking me questions about Casey, about our friendship, what we did together for fun, what her family was like, what she was like outside of school. We had all known Casey since grade three, and everyone in the group had different memories of her. For days, that's all we talked about at the restaurant, each day beginning where we'd left off the day before, as though there had been no interruption.

They asked me if I'd received any more letters from Casey. I didn't answer right away. The fate of the first letter was still too raw.

"You did, didn't you?" Amber said. "How is she doing? Is she falling apart?"

"She's not," I replied. "She's pretty strong."

"Well, of course you're going to say that," said Amber. "Of course you're going to defend her."

"No, really," I said, going into my bag where I kept the letter. "Let me read it to you."

"Not out loud," Amber said, looking around the restaurant. "You don't know who's listening." She reached across the table and took the letter from me.

Somehow, Nathan moved his elbow or something and my glass of Coke toppled over, spilling soda and ice-cubes all over me.

"What a mess!" Nathan said. "That lousy waitress better have some clean towels."

He hustled me toward the counter, helped me mop up, and by the time we got back to the table, Amber and the others were finished with the letter.

"It's all about the bugs with her, isn't it?" Amber said, handing Casey's letter back to me.

"All about the bugs," I agreed, tucking it back into my bag.

The conversation went on to other memories of Casey, and I thought no more about the letter until it also appeared on the front page of the paper two days later.

The Cactus gang didn't mention it, and I couldn't figure out how they could have done anything in the few moments I was drying myself off, so I let it go. It was easier that way.

I kept going to the restaurant with them after school. We ordered our Cokes and plates of French fries with gravy and we talked. I told them everything, every memory I had of Casey, all the fun, secret things we used to do, things that had never gone beyond the two of us. It felt good to talk about her. It felt good to have an attentive audience.

I should have been ashamed to reveal things that Casey would never have told anyone else but me, but I believed I was doing Casey a favor. The restaurant gang would welcome her as one of them when she got out of jail. Casey could sit with us at our table by the window, sharing fries and talking.

I told myself a lot of lies. I could no more picture Casey hanging out with that group than I could picture Reverend Fleet on *American Idol*. Dishonesty is a fungus, I've discovered. Once it settles into your soul, it just keeps growing and clinging to everything.

After two weeks of talking about Casey, I was all out of stories. It was Friday, and near time for us to leave the restaurant. It was comfortable there, with the smell of gravy and bad Chinese food in the air. I was not anxious to leave. An autumn storm was brewing, and life at home was not happy.

"It's been really great talking with you about Casey," Amber said.

"Yeah, very profitable," said Nathan, chuckling.

"He means we've all profited by being able to understand her better," interjected Amber, quickly. "But I have one last question for you."

I waited, playing with my straw. When she didn't ask it right away, I looked up.

Her expression serious, she asked, "Do you think she did it? Do you think Casey killed that girl, little Stephanie? We all think she did it. Do you?"

"No," I replied. "You don't know her like I do. Casey wouldn't do that."

"But say you were on the jury," Amber continued. "What if you were on the jury and you didn't know her, and you'd been told that Stephanie drove her crazy, that Stephanie's bloody t-shirt was found in her bag, and that she walked right by the body when she searched the trail. What if you heard all of that and there were no other suspects? And let's face it—you were not there. You think you know her, but maybe you don't know all of her. Driven to it, we could probably all be killers."

And I said, "In that case, yes, I would have to say that I think Casey is guilty. I think she killed Stephanie."

A strange smile crossed Amber's face. The others were nodding and smiling, too.

I'm embarrassed to admit it now, even to a stranger, but what I felt then was satisfaction. I'd given the right answer. I was still in the group.

Did I believe it? Actually, it didn't much matter to me what I believed. I cared only about being asked back to the group. I was terrified that they'd drop me and I'd be all alone again, facing the world without Casey.

At two a.m., I went into the garage to get my bike. It was gone. Mom must have given it to the Whites. They wouldn't mind if I went over there to get it, even at that hour, but I wasn't about to do that. It was gone. I let it stay gone.

I jogged for a few blocks but it didn't feel the same,

so I went home. I sat down on the cold cement of the garage. I thought about the warm garage at Casey's house, the garage turned bug-den and family room. I put my hand out on the spot where my bike used to be. And I cried.

June 15, 2010

I bike over to Casey's after cross-country. Casey runs down the street to meet me, waving a piece of paper in the air.

"I've been accepted!" she calls out, dancing and running and jumping all at the same time. "I'm going to Australia! Four whole months!"

I smile, because I know I'm supposed to. Four months! I would be without her for four months.

"Here's a picture of it—the True Blue cockroach. Isn't it the most beautiful thing you ever saw?"

She shoves a photo of the ugly thing right in my face. I want to tear into it with my teeth.

"I'll be camping out on Lord Howe Island!" She keeps talking. She hasn't even asked about my day. "I'll be looking for roaches, counting roaches, measuring roaches, cleaning the camp, helping the entomologists, sitting around in the bush at night with a lantern on my head, waiting for them to crawl out of their burrows—the roaches, not the entomologists! Maybe I can help keep the roaches from going extinct! Oh, this is the best day of my life!"

She keeps dancing in the street and waving that damned letter around. One of her neighbors comes out to see what all the excitement is about. While she is talking to him, I walk away.

The best day of Casey's life has nothing to do with me.

She never asks me why I walked away.

She is too busy being happy to care.

EIGHTEEN

The next day, I was dropped from the group.

It was really something, the way they dropped me. I almost have to admire them for it, now. There was no pretense of niceness, no beating about the bush. Just a clear, unequivocal signal that I was persona non grata once again.

After school, I waited at my locker, where the restaurant gang picked me up on the way out of the school, since my locker was the closest one to the door we used. I saw them coming, shut my locker door, snapped the padlock closed, and turned to them with a smile on my face, like a great big grinning idiot.

They walked right by me. No greeting, no sign of recognition. I may as well have been one of those Caution-Wet-Floor signs for all the attention they paid to me.

I fell in behind the group anyway. They closed ranks, like a herd of musk ox protecting itself against intruders.

I followed them out of the school and down the street like a giant goof, saying things like, "Tough history quiz today, huh, Amber?" and "What got into Mr. Higgins?" But no one responded. They didn't even laugh or shove me away. They all simply and completely ignored me. You have to admire that type of discipline.

Eventually, about a half mile from the school, I got the message. I stopped in the middle of the sidewalk and watched the group go on without me, feeling—well, you can imagine what I was feeling.

The plus side of it all was that I was able to start training with the cross-country team after school again. There's nothing like vigorous physical activity to help you get over humiliation. Ms. Simms said nothing to me about my schedule change, other than, "I don't want yo-yo's on my team," which I took to mean I'd better not switch again. No jolly fear of that. So now I could sleep a bit later in the mornings.

But my actions were to have more consequences. It took a few days, but I finally discovered why the restaurant gang had asked me to join them in the first place.

It first showed up on the Internet. I was in the library and passed some kids huddled over a Blackberry.

I heard my voice coming out of it. I leaned in for a closer look.

There I was, sitting in The Cactus, talking about Casey.

They had filmed it, probably with some spy camera. I watched for a few minutes, not even feeling that surprised. Then the show stopped and some words appeared on the screen—to watch the whole interview, people needed to enter their credit card number.

I didn't hang around to see if any of the students were pulling out their wallets.

You probably saw me on one of those scandal shows. The story ran on all the major networks.

After that, a full-page article appeared in the Saturday editions of all the city newspapers. "Friends With a Murderer" it was called, and it was written by none other than Amber Bradley of Galloway District High School.

There were direct quotes in the interview from our conversations at The Cactus, but Amber hadn't stopped there. She'd talked to some of Casey's old teachers, some who had known her since grade school. Miss Burke was quoted as saying Casey was the most promising student she'd ever taught, but this was followed by a paragraph describing Miss Burke's police escort from the school, which weakened the value of her support.

Other kids in the article talked about Casey's so-called weirdness, her obsession with insects, and her lack of boyfriends. But by far the most damning statement came from me. It was even featured in a bold-faced sub-headline: *"I think she killed Stephanie," says Summer Camp Murderer's Best Friend.*

They probably all divided up the money from the article. Amber may have gotten the lion's share because she actually wrote it up. They saw an opportunity to make money, and they took it. If I were to object, they'd band together and insist I knew I was being taped.

I was furious, thinking of them sitting smugly in that restaurant, eating the French fries and drinking the Cokes that my stupidity helped them buy. In my anger, I saw myself storming into The Cactus and dumping those fries and drinks all over their scheming little heads. But of course I didn't do it. I didn't do anything.

Mom was already wound up and crazy by this point, but she was still talking to me, sometimes endlessly. On and on she'd talk about loyalty and friendship and loneliness, often repeating herself as if to drive home the point. Frequently, I would leave the room while she was talking to me, and she'd keep right on talking. I'd go back into the room, and she wouldn't even blink at my return. Or I'd go to bed and hear her talking to herself in the living room, late at night. That was normal. That was just Mom.

But when she saw the article, she gave me a long hard look as though I were someone she ought to recognize but didn't, and stopped speaking to me. Dad wasn't saying much even before that, so our house had become pretty quiet. So it actually took me a couple of days to realize that Mom had stopped talking altogether. I found it eerie. Dad was probably grateful for the silence. I don't know. He never said.

NINETEEN

There was silence at home and silence at school. Now and then, some kid would come up to me and say, "I don't understand how you could do that to Casey. I thought she was your best friend."

The very thing I was most afraid of was the very thing that happened. I was alone. I should have skipped all the intervening nonsense with The Cactus gang and gone straight to the alone part.

Dad and I went along for a few weeks without hearing a word from Mom. It was a relief not to have to listen to her lectures on friendship, but her silence was ominous. It meant she had given up on me. And it meant that she was going to a place where no one could reach her.

I continued to get up at my usual hour in the dead of night, and walk or jog around town until I could face going back to bed. I missed my bike but did nothing to get it back.

Mom was always up when I got back to the house from these night rambles. Sometimes she'd be pacing around the house, or trying to get a big chair out the front door to take to the Whites'. I'd take the chair or whatever it was from her and she'd turn away from me, leaving me to put the chair back beside the living-room sofa. Sometimes she'd just be sitting, staring at me as I came in through the back door. I could feel her eyes on me all the way upstairs until I closed my bedroom door to keep them out. She never said a word.

Dad and I waited for the inevitable crisis.

It came.

I had just gotten back into a sound sleep after one of my rambles when a loud thud woke me up. I was out of bed and down the stairs before my brain even knew I was awake. Dad met up with me in the kitchen. For a long, horrible moment, all we could do was stare.

Mom was on the floor. The refrigerator was on top of her, pinning her down.

I grabbed a corner of the fridge and tried to raise it. My feet swam in a sea of broken eggs, orange juice and other stuff that had spilled out. The refrigerator wouldn't budge.

"Don't," my father said, reaching for the phone.

"Dad, help me!" I urged, but he turned his back on Mom and me and talked into the phone. I knew he was calling the hospital. I knew he was calling to get some one to come and take Mom away.

I tore upstairs and grabbed a pillow from my bed. I bent down to put it under Mom's head.

"Don't," Dad said again, his hand restraining my wrist. "Her spine could be hurt. Don't move her."

I wiped her face with a warm cloth and smoothed the hair out of her eyes.

"Where do you go at night, my Jude?" she asked in a thin voice. "Why don't you ever take me with you?"

I had no answer for her. I just sat on the floor beside her until the paramedics burst into the kitchen.

Dad took me to the other side of the kitchen to give the medics room to work. Their loud, clear, emotionless voices were a comfort. They knew what to do.

"I'll give the fridge to the Whites," Mom said, more to herself than to any of the rest of us.

"This will calm you down, Mrs. Harris," one of the medics said, plunging a needle into her arm. Dad helped them lift the fridge off her. When I saw the state of her legs, I screamed. I couldn't help it.

Dad took me into the living room and wrapped a blanket around my shoulders while the medics got

Mom ready for transport. It took a long time. He made me some instant hot chocolate. I didn't drink it, but the warmth of the mug felt good.

Finally, they had her on the stretcher. They took her out of the house and down the front steps.

"I'm gong to follow them to the hospital," Dad said. "Do you want to come with me or will you be okay here?"

In response, I dashed out of the house and caught up with the medics just as they were lifting Mom into the ambulance.

"Mom!" I cried out.

"Judie? My Judie?" Mom's voice was weak through the pain and the sedative. She reached out and grabbed my hand. "Get out of here, my Jude. Get out of this town. Don't let it do to you what it did to me!"

She appeared to pass out then, her hand suddenly limp in mine. The medics slid her stretcher into place, and I backed away from the ambulance just as the doors were slammed shut.

Dad pulled out of the driveway to follow the ambulance to the hospital, and I went back inside the house. I turned on the television, and I just sat.

Mom's legs were badly hurt. The damage would not be permanent but she had a long road to recovery ahead of her.

"Tissue can mend," the doctor said when Dad and I went to see him. "The bigger worry is her mental state. Don't expect her home anytime soon."

Mom was usually in the hospital for three or four weeks. I couldn't guess how long it would be this time.

Somehow, Dad and I got through Christmas. We avoided it, really. We went to see Mom on Christmas Day, but she wouldn't respond to us, and the false cheeriness of the hospital ward depressed us both. I tried to get caught up on my studying. I rented a lot of old war movies from the video store and spent the holidays watching people get blown up. Dad went to see Mom every night after work, but I never went back.

"Her legs are healing," the doctor said early in January, "but I'm worried about her not speaking. As soon as she's strong enough, we'll start on electroconvulsive therapy again."

It was a relief to be left alone at school. I was glad to be free of The Cactus gang. Trying to keep up with their conversations about nothing would have been a terrible strain.

I missed Mom. I didn't exactly need her for anything. I could look after the house and myself, but I missed somebody taking an interest in whether I'd had a decent breakfast, or whether that shirt was clean enough for one more day. And she was always doing something interesting and trying to drag me into it with her. It used to bug me, but now I missed it.

The craziness around the murder had died down over the holidays, except for a few stories about Stephanie's mom spending Christmas alone. It started up again in the middle of January, as the date for Casey's trial got closer.

On the Thursday before the trial started, I received a letter from Casey.

Dear Dragonfly,

My trial is coming up soon. Mela keeps telling me everything will be fine, but I know it won't be. She had no luck getting the trial moved to another town, but I don't think that would have made much of a difference anyway. A lot of issues are tearing this country apart, but there's one thing everyone agrees on—they all hate me! Do you think I could get a National Unity Award?

Your letters still aren't getting through. I don't understand it. Miss Burke's letters get in. So do Mrs. Keefer's and your mom's. I don't know why they won't let me have your letters.

Sometimes I think horrible things. I think why couldn't I have gone to the hospital with Deanna? Then you would be in here instead of me. I hate myself for thinking such a horrible thing.

I don't know how Stephanie ended up dead, stuffed in that hollow tree, but I don't have an alibi and there are no other suspects, so I don't have much of a chance. I'm going to spend the rest of my life in a cage.

Sorry, this is not a cheerful letter. I heard that your mom is in the hospital again. Please give her my best. Let me know if I can do anything.

Keep sending me letters. Eventually they'll let me read them.

Casey

The next day, I received another letter. This one was a subpoena. I was ordered to be a witness for the prosecution at the trial of my best friend.

TWENTY

The prosecutor called my father to let him know when I had to appear in court. I stayed away from the courthouse until then. I didn't want to see anybody—not the Whites, not Casey, not Mrs. Glass, not anybody.

It was easy to follow the progress of the trial. It was all over the news.

First there was the jury selection, and then the scientists were brought in to testify how Stephanie had been killed. One expert identified Casey's blood and skin tissue under Stephanie's fingernails. Mela asked if the blood could have come from a scratch Stephanie gave Casey earlier and the expert had to admit that, yes, it could. The same expert stated that Casey's hair in the hair clip could have become pulled out at any time, even days before.

The Tinker Bell t-shirt they'd found in Casey's bag was introduced with great flourish, according to a story in one of the newspapers. The paper also described Mrs. Glass "filling the courtroom with the sound of her wracking sobs." A criminal psychologist took the stand to say that many murderers keep a trophy of their crime.

A lot of time was spent examining photos of the tree where Stephanie was found, the prosecution saying Casey would have seen some sign of Stephanie if she had really been looking. Mela said that the leaves and branches clearly made seeing the tree difficult, and that the police hadn't found Stephanie either when they'd searched that area. In fact, Stephanie wasn't found until the rain finally stopped and the search dogs were brought in.

I hated having the events of the summer dredged up in such detail.

The morning of my testimony, I changed clothes five times, from jeans to church dress to in-between and then back to jeans, as if the right clothes could make me feel better about the whole thing.

I had asked Dad to be with me in court when I testified, but he made it so clear that he didn't want to be, just by his expression, that I told him not to bother. I was all alone.

By the time I got to the courthouse, I was so worked up I knew I couldn't do it.

I found the Crown attorney, Mr. Tesler, in the hallway.

"I don't want to testify," I said. "I don't feel well. And I don't have anything to say—really! I don't want to do this!"

"You have a subpoena, a judicial order," he replied. "What you *want* is irrelevant. You will take the stand and you will confirm what's in your signed statement, or you will join your little friend in jail. And don't think I can't put you there because I can." With that, he walked away.

Later that morning, I sat on a bench away from Casey's courtroom but within sight of the door, so that I'd be able to hear the clerk call me in. I was bent over, looking at the floor, when someone spoke to me.

"I knew you'd be here somewhere."

I looked up. It was Mrs. Keefer, the camp director. She sat down beside me.

"You're testifying this afternoon, aren't you?"

I nodded. "How did you know?"

"The prosecutor has to give its witness list to the defense," she said. "I'm testifying later, on Casey's behalf."

I was stricken. "So Casey knows?"

Mrs. Keefer nodded. "Casey knows."

Shame flooded through me. "How can I face her?"

Mrs. Keefer was quiet for a moment. Then she said, "Do you remember the inscription on the plaque in the center of the ten willows?"

"Of course. 'On the willows, we hung up our lyres, for our captors demanded songs, and our tormenters, mirth.'"

"Do you know what it means?"

"No. I don't."

"It means when people who are doing wrong want us to do something to please them, we don't have to do it. We have a choice. We can pack up our lyres and refuse to play."

I looked up at her. "But how—?" I was going to ask her how that applied to me, here and now, but I looked at her face, and I knew. I was drowning in shame, and she was tossing me a lifeline.

She gave me a hug, then left me alone to think.

I thought.

I knew what I had to do. I had to get up on that witness stand, take the oath, look Tesler in the eye, and say, "Casey White is my best friend. She would never kill anybody."

And more. I'd have to tell them more.

That, I knew, I could never do.

Maybe it would be enough to just refuse to play.

Maybe it would be enough to say, "Casey White would never kill anybody and if you can't see that, too bad for you, because that's the truth." Then I'd refuse to say another word.

The prosecutor's case would collapse. Relief would wash over the Whites. Casey would forgive me, my mom would hear about it and get well, and everything would be back to normal. Spring was on the way and we would be happy again.

Over and over, I imagined what I'd do, and how I'd say it. I pictured myself being charged with contempt of court and led out in handcuffs, everyone cheering me. Everyone would like me again. Maybe Mela would even agree to be my lawyer. My body sweated and shivered with adrenalin. By the time lunch recess was over, and the prosecutor's assistant came to fetch me, I was fever-pitch ready.

Then I entered the courtroom.

I seemed to watch myself from a distance, climbing into the witness box, taking the oath on the Bible, sitting down in front of the microphone. I realized then that all eyes were on me. I saw a good chunk of Galloway, including Miss Burke, in the spectator seats. Mr. and Mrs. White were up front. Casey was sitting beside Mela at the defense table. She was wearing a plain blue dress I'd never seen before. She met my gaze. She didn't look mad or hostile, just disappointed. It nearly killed me, to have her look at me like that.

Remember the plan, I told myself. *Just do this one thing, and everything will be all right.*

If I had stood up right then and made my statement, I think I could have salvaged things. People forgive. We could have talked it out.

But Mr. Tesler stepped forward and started asking questions, and I fell into my old obedient behavior. He started easy, asking questions I could answer without thinking: how long had I known Casey, what were our duties at camp, and did Casey have a problem with Stephanie stealing her things. I kept hoping there would be a spot in the questioning where it would be natural for me to do my big, brave thing. Mr. Tesler, as if he could sense my mood, did not give me any opportunity. If my answers went beyond a few words, he jumped in and ordered me to be direct. He didn't give me a chance to expand on anything or add anything of my own.

"How well did you and Casey know the trails at Ten Willows?"

"Very well," I replied. "We'd been going there for years, plus we had permission to be there in the off-season. The Camp Administration trusted Casey especially, and—"

"Stephanie's Tinker Bell t-shirt was found in Casey

White's duffel bag, pushed down among her camp clothes. When asked about it, Ms. White stated that she did not put it there. She also stated that you were asked to clean the cabin and pack up her bag as well as Stephanie's, and you left the search staging area in order to carry out the request. Did you clean the cabin and pack up Casey and Stephanie's belongings?"

"I was asked to, and so I did."

And then he came to the question I'd been dreading.

"Did you put Stephanie Glass's Tinker Bell t-shirt into Casey White's duffel bag?"

There it was.

I suddenly developed a cough. I coughed and coughed and pointed at the pitcher of water on the lawyer's table.

Mr. Tesler frowned at me like he knew I was faking. He took his sweet time pouring me a glass of water and handing it to me. I took my sweet time drinking it, trying to get up the nerve to make my big statement.

"Would you like me to repeat the question?" Mr. Tesler asked.

I nodded.

"Did you put Stephanie Glass's Tinker Bell t-shirt into Casey White's duffel bag?"

Then, just at that moment, just like in a movie, the clerk received a message from a court messenger and handed it to the judge. We all watched him read it.

"Would the attorneys, the defendant, and the defendant's parents please see me in my chambers immediately?"

We all stood as the judge, along with everyone he summoned, left the courtroom. I didn't know what else to do, so I stayed in the witness box. It was awful, sitting up there, where everyone could see me. I could feel myself wilting with each passing minute. I tried to rehearse my big speech, but I felt less and less like delivering it, and more and more like going home.

Half an hour later, the bailiff approached Mrs. Glass and asked her to join the others in the judge's chambers. Twenty minutes after that, they all came back in again. It looked like everyone had been crying. Except for Mr. Tesler and the judge.

Mr. Tesler did not take up his former position in front of me. Instead, he stood behind his table and spoke to the judge.

"Your Honor, in light of new, irrefutable evidence that's been brought to our knowledge, the Crown wishes to drop all charges against Casey White."

The crowd in the courtroom gasped. The judge ignored them.

"Casey White, please stand."

Casey and Mela stood up.

"All charges against you have been dropped. You

are free to go. Case dismissed." He pounded with his gavel and left the courtroom.

No one moved. We were all too stunned.

Then Casey left the defense table and went over to Mrs. Glass. Mrs. Glass rose to meet her. They embraced.

Casey started to cry. "Poor little Stephanie," she sobbed. "Poor little Stephanie."

Casey and Stephanie's mother hugged each other and cried, then Mela and the Whites joined them as they walked out the front door of the courthouse. The people of Galloway slowly filed out of the spectator seats. I don't know if any of them spoke to Casey or not. Nobody spoke to me. I remained where I was. I sat in that witness box, all alone in the courtroom until a janitor turned off the lights and ordered me out.

By that time, there was no one left outside.

TWENTY-ONE

Of course you know now what had happened to stop the trial, but we didn't know until hours later, when we saw it on the news.

The man who killed Stephanie got careless. In the town of Kitchener, a few days before the end of Casey's trial, he tried to grab a girl coming out of her Girl Guide meeting. The little girl started screaming, and a flock of Guides flew out of the church and surrounded him. They hung onto him, dragged him down, and blew their whistles until help came running.

The Girl Guides became heroes. They got a national medal of bravery and appeared on all the TV shows. You probably saw all that.

The cops impounded the man's car, where they found a t-shirt Stephanie had stolen from me and I had never missed. It was the shirt she was wearing when she was killed. It had her blood on it and hairs from the guy's head on it. They also found clothing belonging to a kid he had murdered in Windsor. He confessed to both murders and his confession checked out.

He had been lying in wait for us, hiding in the forest on the edge of the camp, waiting for his best chance. He grabbed Stephanie because she was a little bit apart from the group, so she was the easiest to get to. He hit her on the head while she was sleeping so she made no noise when he took her away.

There was no real reason why he did it. He chose Ten Willows by chance; he chose Stephanie by chance. It wasn't personal. He just liked killing kids. Some men are like that.

I never had to answer Mr. Tesler's question.

I still don't know how I would have answered it.

Because of course I shoved Stephanie's t-shirt into Casey's bag.

I'd been searching for the little brat for hours. I kept trying to talk Casey into sneaking away with me, going to hide out in an empty cabin or even walk home through the rain, but she wouldn't. She even almost snapped at me.

"She's just a little kid," she said. "She could have fallen. She could be hurt. We can't stop looking just because we're tired and wet."

And she flounced away from me, back into the woods.

I started grumbling so much and so loudly that Mrs. Keefer suggested I go back to my cabin and pack up Stephanie's belongings as well as Casey's and my things.

Casey's stuff was already mostly packed. All the other campers were gone. I packed up my things then packed up Stephanie's. I took Stephanie's bag up to the dining hall where her mother could pick it up. Then I went back to my cabin to sweep.

I found the Tinker Bell t-shirt when I was sweeping under the bunks.

I didn't feel like hauling it all the way back to the dining hall. I looked at my bag and I looked at Casey's and I looked at the garbage pail.

If I put the shirt in the garbage pail, someone might see it there and ask why I'd thrown it away, and that would have been a hassle.

If I put it in my bag then I'd have to either get it to Stephanie or dispose of it at my house. Both seemed like too much work.

So I put it in Casey's bag. It was the easiest.

I should have thrown it in the woods or left it on the floor.

I never should have been asked to deal with it in the first place. It wasn't my t-shirt. It shouldn't have been my problem.

Casey was back in school the following Monday. The halls buzzed with the news of her return.

I didn't actually see her until lunchtime, but first I encountered The Cactus gang. They pushed their way to the front of the cafeteria checkout line with an arrogance that told me they weren't the least ashamed about what they'd done.

"I see your girlfriend is back in school," Amber Bradley said.

"Probably thinks she's some kind of hero," said Nicole, poking me in the back. "Probably thinks the school will welcome her with open arms."

"That's not going to happen," Nathan added.

"Why are you saying this to me?" I asked.

"Just in case you two have any notions of picking up where you left off," Amber replied. "We don't want that sort of thing at Galloway High. Casey may or may not be a murderer, but she is still weird, isn't she?"

The group pushed past me into the cafeteria.

"So you just get away with it?" I called after them.

Amber came back and stood two inches from my

face. "Get away with what?"

"Everything. Trashing her house, making money off those lies—everything."

"*You're* getting away with it," Amber replied, a nasty smirk on her face. "Casey was fair game to us. She was never our friend. We never cared about her. What's your excuse?" With that, she turned away and rejoined her friends.

Casey came in while I was having my lunch. She walked toward an empty table, her lunch tray in her hands. The cafeteria went silent.

The Cactus gang blocked her way.

"We don't want you in our school." Amber's voice was loud and clear and mean.

Casey tried to move through them, but they knocked the lunch tray out of her hands. The sound of the dishes crashing to the floor made us all jump.

For a moment, no one moved.

Then I saw Casey do the most extraordinary thing I've ever seen anyone do. She held her hands out in front of her as if she were still holding the lunch tray, and began walking again toward the tables. The Cactus gang parted and let her pass.

She surveyed the room, her eyes resting on me for a brief second, then moving on. She found a vacant seat at another table, sat down, and pretended to eat her lunch. She was calm, unhurried, and unafraid.

That's when I knew that Casey had already left Galloway. Oh, she'll be there until she finishes high school, but the town can't touch her anymore. Amber's meanness, the church's pettiness, even my disloyalty—none of that mattered to her. Nothing we did could hurt her, ever again. She had beaten us all.

Watching her, I was overtaken by the depth of what I had lost, of the friend I'd thrown away because I didn't have the courage to stand by her. Loneliness overpowered me, and I could barely breathe.

I couldn't stand it. I jumped out of my seat and ran from the cafeteria. I stopped at my locker only long enough to grab my coat. At home, I threw some things into my mother's car and I started to drive.

"Get out of this town," Mom had implored, and, for once, I was doing as she'd asked.

That was nearly five months ago. I had meant to go far away, maybe to Arizona, but I couldn't seem to get more than fifty miles away from Galloway. I drifted for a while, picking up cash here and there for this and that, and then I landed at the Roach House.

I phone Dad every now and then. He wasn't surprised that I'd left. Mom's the same, he says. He doesn't know when she'll be coming home.

There was a letter from Casey waiting for me in the mailbox the day I left home. She must have mailed it a few days before I testified, when it still looked like she'd be spending her life in prison. She wrote:

Dear Jess,

Mela finally told me that you are going to testify against me, and I'm writing to tell you that it doesn't matter.

I would have been hurt by it, except that just after she told me, a cockroach wandered into my cell. I took one look at it, and I automatically knew it was an American cockroach, of the order Blattodea, family Blattidae, one of six hundred species worldwide. I knew its Latin name, *Periplaneta Americana*, and I knew that the females produce up to fifty egg cases, each holding a dozen eggs.

I reminded myself that I'm the same person, in or out of prison. There are bugs everywhere, and my life, my passion, my self, will not be ruined unless I let it be ruined.

I did not kill Stephanie, but I did fall asleep, allowing Death to come in the night and take her from us, before she had a chance to stop being annoying and become the person she was meant to be. I'll have to live with that forever. But I didn't kill her. And I will find happiness, and meaning, even in the penitentiary.

I don't know why you allowed the world to change you, Dragonfly. You used to have such courage.

Casey

Casey was wrong about me, you know. I never had courage.

If I were courageous, I'd drive on back to Galloway and try to make things right with her again. But how can I do that? How can I prove to her that I'm someone who deserves to have her for a friend?

Mom would know. If I could talk to Mom, she'd tell me what I should do. If I could get her away from that hospital, get those awful drugs out of her system, I could convince her that I've changed, and she'd help me win Casey back. Casey trusts her. And Mom knows how hard it was on me to live in that town. And what I went through while Casey was in detention.

I could really do that, you know. I could drive up to the hospital in the morning, as soon as I got off shift. I can go up to her ward during visiting hours, so my presence wouldn't look suspicious. I can take some extra clothes with me, get her out of that hospital gown they probably have her wearing, then take her calmly down the elevator and put her into the car.

We can even come back here to the Roach House for a few days. There's a storeroom in the back she can sleep in, just until the drugs wear off and she can call Casey.

"Come out here and join us," she'll say to Casey. "My brave daughter gave me my life back. Come out here and we'll drive to Arizona and get away from everyone!"

And Casey will come because she loves my mother and she loves me, and everything will be back to the way it used to be.

Back when we were friends.

QUESTIONS FOR DISCUSSION

1. How would you describe Jess as the narrator of the story? Did you trust her interpretation of events? Would you consider her to be a reliable or unreliable narrator?

2. Why do you think Jess lied to Detective Bowen about the Tinker Bell shirt? When asked about the shirt in court, Jess is about to answer but the session is interrupted. What do you think she would have said?

3. Do you think Jess thought Casey was guilty? Did you ever think Casey was guilty? Did you ever suspect Jess?

4. What did you think of Stephanie Glass? Do you think it was a reasonable decision to keep Jess and Casey in charge of Stephanie after the first signs of trouble? How else could the camp have handled Stephanie?

5. What was your reaction when Jess describes the praying mantis signal in the first scene? Why do you think Casey sent Jess the signal in court?

6. Describe Jess and Casey's relationship. How did their friendship change during this story?

7. How does Jess see her mother? Do you think she is viewed in the same way by Casey and her family? What about the people in the nursing home?

8. How might her mother's mental illness influence Jess and her relationship with others?

9. Why did Jess's mother want to bring Casey's family so many objects from her own home? Why do you think she was so upset by Casey's arrest?

10. Why was Ten Willows such a special place for Casey and Jess? Do you think it held the same meaning for both girls?

11. How would you describe The Cactus gang? Why did Jess want to be friends with them?

12. Do you think Jess decided to turn on Casey? If so, at what point did she make the decision?

13. What do you think of Miss Burke and her decision to blockade herself in the office? Do you think she expected a different outcome?

14. Do you think Casey and Jess could repair their friendship? Would Casey want to?

15. Choose one decision that either Casey or Jess made that you would have done differently. How might that have changed the story?

16. What do you think Casey might be doing five years after this story ends? What about Jess? The Cactus gang?

17. Why do you think the author titled the book *True Blue*?